THE NANCY DREW FILES™

Case 6

POISON PEN

CAROLYN KEENE

AN ARCHWAY PAPERBACK
Published by POCKET BOOKS
New York London Toronto Sydney Tokyo Singapore

AN ARCHWAY PAPERBACK *Original*

An Archway Paperback published by
POCKET BOOKS, a division of Simon & Schuster
1230 Avenue of the Americas, New York, NY 10020

ISBN: 0-671-70037-5

First Archway Paperback printing June 1991

10 9 8 7 6 5 4 3 2 1

Cover art by Tom Galasinski

Printed in the U.S.A.

IL 7+

POISON PEN

Chapter

One

MMM, this is the life," Nancy Drew said with a contented sigh. She draped her fluffy rainbow-striped towel at the foot of the lounge chair and sank down into the soft cushions. Her reddish blond hair spread out around her head like a halo, glowing in the bright sunlight. "Nothing beats a long, lazy day at the River Heights Country Club pool."

"Don't I know it," agreed her friend Bess Marvin. Bess was stretched out on the lounge chair next to Nancy's, her eyes closed and her fair skin glistening with sunscreen. "Don't you wish summer would last forever?"

"Not me," piped up Bess's cousin George Fayne from the other side of Nancy. "I'd hate to give up skiing." Leaning on one elbow, she ran her fingers through her short, dark curls, which were still wet from swimming. "But don't worry, Bess. It's only June. We've still got the whole summer in front of us!"

"With heat like this, it's hard to believe the summer is just beginning," Nancy commented. "I heard the temperature was supposed to hit ninety today." She plucked at the fabric of her neon green two-piece bathing suit. "I think it's about there now, and I think I'm almost ready to jump in the pool."

Bess opened her eyes and stared gravely at first Nancy and then George. "Tornado weather," she said with a shudder. Her gaze drifted lazily in front of Nancy, but then her blue eyes suddenly flew open wide. "Hey, Nancy," she said in an urgent whisper. "Who is that *gorgeous* guy?"

"Gorgeous guy?" George repeated, sitting up straight. "Where?"

"Over there," Bess said, gesturing.

Shading her eyes with her hand, Nancy gazed over at the other side of the pool, where a young man of about nineteen or twenty had just settled into the lifeguard's chair. He had shining black hair and classic chiseled features. His skin was tanned to a deep, glowing brown, which emphasized his slim yet muscular build. He was talking with a tall, lanky blond guy who stood by the chair.

"You mean the guy in the chair or the guy next to it?" George asked. "They're both pretty awesome looking, if you ask me. Hey—doesn't the tall one look familiar?"

"I can't believe you don't recognize David Park and Jonathan Evans," Nancy said, shaking her head. "They were only a year ahead of us in high school."

"That's David Park?" Bess whispered. "That dark-haired hunk is the skinny, quiet guy who used to work in the library?"

"The one and only," Nancy replied, laughing.

"Jonathan Evans!" George seemed flabbergasted. "Boy, has he changed."

"Yeah, they both blossomed late," Nancy agreed. "I guess I shouldn't be teasing you about not recognizing them. I might not have known them myself, except that they go to Emerson College now. They're friends of Ned's."

Bess's eyebrows shot up. "Well, why didn't you say so? You can reintroduce us."

"Good idea, Bess," George put in, her brown eyes still focused on the two guys.

"Fine by me. They're really nice." Nancy swung her long legs over the edge of her lounge chair and stood up. "Let's go!"

The girls made a striking trio as they walked around the pool to the lifeguard's station. Nancy was slender and lithe, with shoulder-length reddish blond hair and sparkling deep blue eyes. George was a bit taller than Nancy, with dark eyes and curls and the streamlined build of a natural athlete. Petite, curvy Bess had long blond hair, blue eyes, and a flirtatious smile.

"George, does my hair look ratty?" Nancy heard Bess whisper next to her.

"How could it? All you've done since we got here is brush it," George replied.

"That's not true!" Bess began indignantly.

Nancy chuckled as she listened to them argue. Bess and George were almost complete opposites, despite being cousins. One loved sports, the other hated exercise. One was quiet and a little on the shy side, the other bubbly and outgoing. And yet they were practically inseparable. They bickered some, but Nancy knew that under it all they were the best of friends.

"Hi, David. Hi, Jonathan," Nancy called as she approached the lifeguard's station.

The guys glanced over, and David broke into a wide grin of recognition. "Hey!" he greeted her. "How've you been, Nancy? Where's Ned? I haven't seen him since the end of spring semester."

Nancy shrugged. "I wish I saw more of him, too," she admitted. "But Ned's been really busy with his summer job at the insurance company."

"We know what that's like," Jonathan chimed in. He adopted an exaggerated, martyrlike expression and said, "We lifeguards have it pretty tough, sitting out here day after day in the hot sun."

"My heart bleeds for you," Nancy said dryly. Then she gestured toward Bess and George. "You remember Bess Marvin and George Fayne, don't you?"

David's dark eyes sparkled with interest as he took in the cousins, but Nancy noticed that his gaze lingered longer on Bess. "Well, if I didn't, I sure won't forget them now," David declared. "You three look great!"

"George Fayne?" Jonathan gazed at George, and Nancy saw a glint of recognition and then admiration in his eyes. "You were on the school tennis team, right?"

George nodded, her eyes bright. "That's right. And you were the track team's star sprinter."

Nice work, Drew, Nancy congratulated herself. "Hey," she said suddenly as an idea struck her, "are you guys going to the concert at the lake tomorrow night?"

"You bet," Jonathan replied. "Ice Planet's the greatest."

"Well, I'm having a barbecue at my house—just Ned, Bess, George, and me. Why don't you guys come? We can all go to the concert together afterward," Nancy suggested, glancing at Bess and George with a hint of a smile.

"I'll be there," Jonathan said immediately.

"Count me in," David said at the same time.

"Great!" Nancy said. "Come over around six. See you then."

As the girls walked back to their lounges, George whispered to Nancy, "You never said anything to us about a barbecue at your house tomorrow night."

Nancy's blue eyes gleamed mischievously as she explained, "That's because I didn't think of it until just now!"

"That's what I call good thinking." Bess nodded her approval.

Nancy was just lying back on her lounge when Bess demanded in a horrified tone, "Hey, what do you think you're doing?"

"Well, last time I checked, it wasn't a federal crime to lie in the sun," Nancy said, gazing quizzically at Bess. "But I have a feeling that's not what you have in mind."

"You've got that right," Bess retorted. "Come on, you two, get out of those chairs and stop being lazy. We have work to do!" She grabbed Nancy's hand and pulled her to her feet. "The concert's tomorrow night, we're going with three gorgeous guys, and I for one have nothing to wear. We've got to shop!"

"Okay, we're getting there. All I need is a pair of pants to go with the top I just bought," Bess announced. "And maybe—"

"Here we go," George muttered. "And maybe some new shoes, and some new makeup, and a dress in case the top and pants don't look good—"

Nancy laughed. "You should talk," she said, pointing at the bulging shopping bag in George's hand. "You did pretty well yourself."

It was afternoon and the girls had just left Vanities, a trendy boutique at the River Heights mall. Suddenly a familiar, gloating voice rang out from behind them: "Well, if it isn't Nancy Drew."

Even before she looked, Nancy knew who the speaker was: Brenda Carlton, girl reporter and major nuisance. Brenda's father owned *Today's Times,* one of River Heights's daily newspapers. He occasionally let Brenda write articles for the paper, and this had given her the idea that she was an ace crime reporter.

That in itself wasn't so bad. The real problem was that Brenda constantly tried to show Nancy up by meddling in her investigations—often landing herself and Nancy in hot water.

Just recently Nancy had been working to clear Ned of a murder charge, and Brenda's constant interference had almost landed Ned behind bars for life! And to top it off the reporter had had nerve enough to write an article for the paper in which she'd taken credit for solving the case! Needless to say, Brenda wasn't exactly on Nancy's list of her favorite people.

Nancy sighed and turned around with a smile in place. The reporter was wearing a beige silk blouse, tailored slacks, and pumps, and her dark hair was twisted into a French braid. Nancy had to admit she looked very pretty.

"Don't tell me you girls were actually shopping at Vanities," Brenda said with disdain.

"Hi, Brenda," Nancy said in a neutral voice.

George leaned close to Nancy and said in a low voice, "She's probably just jealous. Her dad must have taken away her credit cards this week."

Nancy saw a flash of annoyance in Brenda's dark eyes. "I heard that," Brenda said. "For your information, my cash flow is fine. In fact, I was hoping you three would let me treat you to a late lunch at the Eatery—if you haven't eaten already."

Nancy, Bess, and George exchanged startled glances. Brenda wasn't exactly known for her generosity—especially toward them. Nancy couldn't help wondering if she was up to something.

There was only one way to find out. "Uh, sure. We haven't eaten yet. That'd be nice," Nancy answered.

The four girls took the escalator up to the Eatery, a cafeteria-style restaurant on the mezzanine level. After going through the line, they carried their trays over to an empty table and sat down.

Nancy swallowed a bite of her chicken salad sandwich. "So, Brenda, what's up?" she asked.

Brenda's face radiated an innocence Nancy knew not to trust. "Up? Nothing's up. I was just wondering what kind of plans you have for the summer."

"Oh, I don't know," Nancy said guardedly. "I'm between cases at the moment. I don't really have any special plans."

Bess laughed. "My plan is to have as much fun as possible," she said.

"Mm-hm. Well, I don't think *I'll* have too much time for fun and relaxation," Brenda said, shooting Nancy a significant look.

Here it comes, Nancy thought. "Uh—why not, Brenda?" she asked, taking the bait.

Brenda leaned forward. "I've been given a very important assignment at the paper," she said in a confidential tone.

"Oh!" Bess exclaimed. "You mean your new column. I saw it the other day."

"What column?" Nancy asked, surprised.

"If you ever read a paper, you'd know," Brenda snapped. Then, with a smile at Bess, she added, "At least *you* seem to be concerned about current affairs. So how do you like the column?"

"Well, I've—uh—only seen it once or twice," she answered, sounding a bit embarrassed. She turned to Nancy and George. "Brenda's writing an advice-to-the-lovelorn column," Bess explained. "So far I've seen only one column, though, and it seemed as if there weren't many people who needed advice."

Brenda's cheeks flamed with color. "Yes, there are!" she cried. "The letters have been pouring in. I just—I just haven't had a chance to answer them yet. I've been busy with other important assignments."

Nancy stifled a laugh. The last story of Brenda's she'd seen was on the theft of twelve dollars from the Elks' Lodge petty cash box. Now, that was hot news! Aloud she merely said, "I'm sure more letters will come in, Brenda. People are always getting their hearts broken, falling in love."

"Well, Nancy Drew," Brenda snapped, "it may surprise you to know there are secrets in River Heights that even *you* haven't heard of."

There she goes again, trying to show me up, Nancy thought with a sigh. "I'm sure there are," Nancy returned. "People are bound to have concerns that no one else knows about— or *should* know about. Some matters are just private."

Brenda glared at her. "But there are some things that shouldn't be kept secret, don't you agree?" she retorted.

"Like what?" Nancy asked, picking up her sandwich to take a bite.

"Like murder."

"What? What do you mean?" Nancy demanded, her eyes open wide.

Brenda folded her arms and leaned back in her chair, a satisfied smile on her lips. "I mean—when was the last time *you* got a letter from someone who's afraid they're going to be murdered?"

Chapter

Two

"Murdered?" Nancy repeated, feeling dazed. She put her sandwich down on her plate. "What are you talking about? Who's going to be murdered? Brenda, this could be serious."

"It's nothing for you to worry about," Brenda replied secretively.

"Brenda, are you saying that you got a letter from someone who fears for his or her life? Who is it?" Nancy pressed, leaning forward on her arms.

"None of your business," Brenda retorted. "A reporter never reveals her sources. Anyway, I don't have time to discuss this right now—I have places to go and people to see." She slid her chair back and stood up.

"Wait!" Nancy cried, but Brenda just smiled down at her and grabbed her purse.

"I'm sure I'll see you around town," she said, and flounced away.

The three girls stared after her. Then Bess turned to George and Nancy and asked, "You don't think she's serious, do you?"

"It *would* be just like her to make up something like that," George said, forking a tomato from her chef's salad. "Brenda will do anything for attention."

"That's true," Nancy said slowly. "I'm not sure what to think. Let's go over to the newsstand and check out this column of hers."

Bess and George agreed. After finishing their lunches, the three girls wandered down to a newsstand on the main level. Nancy bought a copy of *Today's Times,* and the girls sat down on a polished wooden bench to read it.

"'Tornadoes Ravage Chicago Suburb,'" George read aloud, peering over Nancy's shoulder at the headline on the front page. "That's awful."

"Yeah. Some friends of my parents live in that town," Bess commented. "They lost their garage."

"They're lucky it was only the garage," Nancy said soberly. "I mean, that's bad, but just think how much worse it could have been. Look at this photo." She pointed at a grainy black-and-white shot of the ruins of a house. One wall was oddly intact, but the rest had totally collapsed.

"Twenty-seven families have been left

homeless," George murmured, still reading the article. "Those poor people!"

"It's this weather," Nancy murmured. "All this awful, heavy heat. Tornadoes breed in it."

Bess blew out her breath in a long sigh. "Please, you guys, let's change the subject," she begged. "All this stuff about tornadoes scares me."

"At least there's no tornado watch set for River Heights yet," Nancy said.

"Well, actually, there was one of those minitornadoes—what do you call them, microbursts—here last weekend," George said. She pointed at some scaffolding set up near one end of the mall's main concourse. "Right over there. It barely touched down. Luckily for the mall, the only damage was to a skylight—oh, and the roof was ripped up a little bit."

Bess looked as if she'd rather be anyplace but where she was right then. "I wish you hadn't told me that, George," she said nervously. Then she gasped. "Oh, no! I just thought of something *really* awful! What if there's a tornado watch tomorrow night? They might call off the concert!"

"Well, there's nothing we can do about it," Nancy pointed out. "Come on, let's read Brenda's column." She flipped through the paper until she came to the Lifestyles section. "Here it is—'Just Ask Brenda.'"

Bess leaned in to get a better look. "Hey, that's a great picture of her."

Nancy peered at the photo. Brenda had a sweet, helpful smile on her face. "I've never seen her look like that in real life," she commented, laughing.

"Read us the first letter, Nan," George suggested. "Let's see what terrible problems Brenda is tackling today."

"Okay, here goes." Nancy went on to read a long, whiny complaint about a neighbor's overgrown, unkempt lawn. "'I have asked her repeatedly to do something about her unsightly property, but she ignores me. What can I do?'" Glancing at Bess and George, Nancy told them, "The letter's signed, 'Fed Up.'"

"Whew!" George exclaimed. "What a boring letter! Are there any others?"

Nancy scanned the column. "Just one. It's from a girl who wants to break up with her boyfriend because the only place he ever takes her is the video arcade."

"What's Brenda's advice?" Bess asked.

"Brenda says it's probably because the girl isn't very interesting," Nancy replied.

George let out a low whistle. "Talk about unsympathetic!"

"Yeah," Bess added. "I think this column would be the last place anyone would turn to if they *really* needed help."

George nodded her agreement. "She was

probably making up what she said just now about someone being afraid."

"If anything exciting ever does appear in this column," said Nancy, tapping the folded-up paper in her lap, "I bet it will be right out of the overactive imagination of Brenda Carlton."

Nancy got up from the bench and dropped the newspaper into a nearby garbage can. "Come on, guys, let's get out of here. I want to get home and see if I can talk Hannah into making something wonderful for dessert for tomorrow night."

"But I never bought a pair of pants," Bess objected.

"Oh, come on," George scolded. "You already have at least ten pairs of pants at home that would look perfect with your new top."

Bess considered for a moment. "Yeah, I guess I do," she agreed. "Okay."

The three girls picked up their shopping bags and headed out to the parking lot to Nancy's blue Mustang. Nancy was the first one through the doors that led from the mall out to the asphalt lot. Heat struck her in a searing wave, and she could feel perspiration bead on her brow.

Suddenly, from somewhere to her right, a sharp screech of rubber tore through the summer air, followed by the loud crashing of metal on metal.

"What was that?" George cried.

Nancy was already running toward the noise. She didn't even turn around as she yelled back, "It sounded like an accident. Come on! Someone might need our help!"

Chapter

Three

As NANCY SPRINTED toward the sound, she could see a crowd gathering around two cars in the parking lot. One of the cars, a silver sedan, had apparently struck the other, a red sports car, on the left front fender.

As Nancy ran up, the driver of the sedan was just climbing out of her car. The woman was about forty, with short ash blond hair, and was wearing an expensive-looking linen suit. Nancy was relieved to see that the woman didn't appear to be injured, although she seemed to be shaken.

Nancy's eyes widened when she saw who the driver of the other car was. Brenda Carlton— and she looked furious.

"Look what you did to my car!" Brenda raged, pointing at her dented front fender. "Don't think you won't pay for the damage!"

18

"I'm so sorry!" the woman exclaimed. Her voice shook, and there were tears in her eyes.

The poor woman sounded as if she was about to break down. Stepping forward, Nancy asked, "Can I help? Is everyone all right?"

"Just barely, no thanks to her," Brenda said, jerking a thumb at the blond-haired woman. "She steered right into me!"

"I tried to stop, really I did," the other woman said shakily. "I kept pumping the brakes, but the car wouldn't—" She broke off with a sob.

"That's crazy!" Brenda declared. "You just weren't paying attention. Someone call the police!"

"I think someone already went to do that," George put in.

"P-police?" The woman's voice quavered. "Oh, dear!"

"Don't worry," Nancy told her, putting an arm around her shoulders and steering her away from Brenda. "It's just routine. The police have to be informed so that they can make a report to your insurance companies. You look pretty shaken up," she went on. "Why don't you sit in your car until the police get here? Here, let me help you."

"Thank you so much," the woman said gratefully. "I'm Mrs. Keating—Maggie Keating. I just don't know what happened," she went on as Nancy led her to the sedan. "I couldn't stop. It was so frightening!"

"I'm sure it was," Nancy said, trying to soothe her. "You should probably have your brakes checked."

"Yes, I'll do that," Mrs. Keating agreed.

Nancy settled Mrs. Keating in the driver's seat, then straightened up to find herself gazing into an extraordinary pair of eyes. One was a deep, vivid blue; the other was golden brown.

The effect was so startling Nancy nearly jumped. The eyes belonged to a muscular, handsome man of medium height, who was standing only a few feet away. He had curly, light brown hair and a square jaw. His face was creased by a slight grin as he stared, first at Nancy, then at Mrs. Keating. Then, turning, the man stepped back into the crowd and was gone.

"Nan, what's wrong?" came Bess's voice.

Blinking, Nancy turned back to her two friends. "Nothing, really," she told them. "It's just that there was an unusual-looking guy here. He had one blue eye and one brown eye. . . ." She let her voice trail off. "I don't know why he seemed so odd, though," she said at last.

"One blue eye and one brown eye? Sounds very unusual to me," George commented. "Like a villain from a romance novel."

"Or a hero," Bess put in. "Was he cute?"

Nancy laughed. "He was pretty good-looking but definitely older. Close to thirty, I'd say."

20

"Nancy! I hope Ned doesn't hear about this," George said in a mock disapproving voice. "I can't believe you're talking with strange older men in parking lots."

"Here comes a patrol car," Bess cut in, pointing toward the entrance to the mall parking lot. "Do you think they'll need us as witnesses or anything?"

"We should probably stick around, just in case," Nancy said. She threw a quick glance at Brenda, who was now regaling the crowd with a dramatic, blow-by-blow account of the crash. "If the police don't get any story besides Brenda's, poor Mrs. Keating might end up in prison for life!"

"I don't believe this," Nancy muttered to herself the following morning. She had gone out after breakfast to pick up a copy of *Today's Times*. Now, as she scanned the opening sentences of "Just Ask Brenda," her eyes widened in amazement. The column had certainly taken a turn for the dramatic since the day before.

Nancy's father Carson Drew had already left for his law office, but Hannah Gruen, the Drews' housekeeper, looked up from the plant she was repotting by the kitchen sink. A pleasant-faced middle-aged woman with graying brown hair and warm eyes, she had lived with the Drews since shortly after the death of Nancy's mother, when Nancy was three. "What don't you believe?" Hannah asked.

Nancy was about to read to her from Brenda's column when the doorbell rang. "I'll get it," she offered. Still holding her copy of *Today's Times,* Nancy went to the foyer.

"Hi, beautiful," a warm male voice greeted her after she threw open the front door.

"Ned!" Nancy's heart leapt with pleasure as she took in her boyfriend's tall, broad-shouldered frame and handsome face. "What are you doing here? Aren't you supposed to be working?"

"I am working," Ned replied, stepping inside. "I had to come into River Heights to pick up some papers, but they won't be ready for another half hour. So I thought I'd come visit my favorite detective. Hey, don't I get a kiss?"

In answer Nancy put the paper down on the hall table and threw her arms around Ned's neck. "You asked for it," she warned, then gave him a warm, lingering kiss.

"Mmm. How about seconds?" he murmured when their lips finally parted.

Nancy ruffled his brown hair and chided, "Don't be greedy!" Then she picked up the newspaper and led the way into the living room.

"What's going on? You don't usually read that rag, do you?" Ned asked, catching sight of the *Today's Times* logo.

"Not usually," Nancy agreed. "But Brenda Carlton has a new column, and I wanted to check it out. Here, take a look." She handed Ned the paper, still opened to Brenda's column, and pulled him down beside her on the couch.

He glanced at it briefly. "What is this, some kind of advice column?"

"Uh-huh," Nancy told him, nodding. "The previous column I read was pretty silly stuff, but this one seems to be spiced up with some 'creative' writing."

Nancy told him about running into Brenda and how Bess had teased her about the column being a little dull. "She got mad and hinted that things were going to get more exciting soon. Lo and behold, the first letter in her column today is from a girl who thinks her mother is going insane. And listen to the second one!"

She took the paper back from Ned and read, "'Dear Brenda, I turn to you in fear and desperation. Please help me. I think my husband is trying to kill me!'"

"What?" Ned exclaimed, alarm in his brown eyes.

Nancy read on.

"It started several weeks ago, when I opened a kitchen cabinet and a heavy silver platter fell from the top shelf and just missed my head. I don't usually keep the silver in that cabinet! What if he put it there hoping it would fall and kill me?

"A week later I was climbing a ladder to prune our apple tree, and my foot slipped on one of the metal rungs. I nearly fell. When I checked the rung, I found it was covered with grease!

"Two days ago I went out to the garage and found my husband under my car with a pair of pliers in his hand. He says he was adjusting the steering, but I'm not sure I believe him. I haven't driven my car since, and I know he wonders why.

"Brenda, I don't know why he's doing this, but I'm sure my suspicions of him are right. I have no one else to turn to. Tell me what to do!

"Desperate."

"I see what you mean," Ned said slowly. "She definitely could have made up something like this. So what's her advice?"

"It's not very good, in my opinion. She tells Desperate to sit tight and do nothing." Nancy pursed her lips. "My advice in this situation would be to tell the woman to go to the police."

Ned gave her a probing look. "But I thought you said you didn't think this letter was real?"

Nancy pressed her lips together. "It would be pretty sleazy—even for Brenda—to lie about something as serious as murder," she said after a moment. "But I guess I wouldn't put it past her. In fact, I think I know where Brenda got the idea for the last part of the letter—the bit about the car, I mean." Nancy told him about the accident in the mall parking lot.

"Brenda was in a fender bender, huh?" Ned remarked.

Nancy nodded. "And Mrs. Keating—the woman in the other car—claimed her brakes weren't working properly," she explained. "I'll bet you anything that's what gave Brenda the idea about the husband sabotaging the car."

"I don't want to bet," Ned said, grinning at her. "I'm sure you're right. Now, stop thinking like a detective for a second and tell me about tonight."

"Okay." Nancy told Ned about the barbecue she'd planned for before the concert.

"So you and I are playing matchmaker, eh?" Ned said. "Sounds like fun!" Glancing at his watch, he added, "Hey, I've got to go. My half hour is almost up." He got to his feet. "Listen, I'll see you tonight."

"I'll be counting the hours, dahling," Nancy said, waggling her eyebrows at him. Then she jumped up and planted a quick kiss on his lips.

"You're a lunatic," Ned said affectionately.

After he left, Nancy spent a couple of hours making potato salad and marinating chicken for the barbecue. Then, at noon, she headed over to the mall to meet George and Bess for some last-minute accessory shopping before the concert.

"What are you going to wear tonight, Nan?" George asked as they walked down the mall concourse.

"I think my aqua dress—you know, the one with the palm trees and flamingoes on it," Nancy replied. "I'd like to find some really fun earrings to go with it, too."

"Let's go to Zigzag," Bess suggested. "They have the best jewelry."

As they approached the little store, Nancy was surprised to see a familiar dark-haired figure moving toward them. "Brenda Carlton —two days in a row," she murmured. "Just our luck."

"Hello, you three," Brenda called. She stepped around the scaffolding in the middle of the concourse and gave it a disapproving glare. "Seen the newspapers this morning?" she chirped.

"If you mean, did we read your column, I did," Nancy replied.

"So did I," Bess spoke up. A troubled expression crossed her face. "Are you sure you gave that woman the right advice, Brenda? I mean, if her husband really is trying to kill her, wouldn't it be wiser for her to go to the police?"

Brenda couldn't keep the satisfied smile off her face. "That shows what you know," she said smugly. "Going to the police wouldn't help anything. I'm handling it."

"Oh," Bess said in an uncertain voice.

"Bess is right," Nancy declared. "If someone came to me with a problem like that, I'd definitely tell her to go to the police." She studied Brenda silently. "On the other hand, *I* don't have a newspaper column to spice up."

Brenda's nostrils flared with anger. "Just what are you trying to say?"

"You tell me," Nancy said evenly.

Suddenly Brenda tossed her head. "You're just jealous because my client didn't come to you, Nancy." She drew herself up haughtily. "If you must know, in tomorrow's column I'm going to tell this woman to get in touch with me. *I'll* get to the bottom of this case. After all, it's the least I can do—the woman asked for my help."

Then Brenda whirled around and marched away.

Staring after her, Nancy said, "I shouldn't have baited her. Now she's going to use her column to prove how great she is at solving a problem, which she probably made up in the first place. This whole dumb thing could go on forever."

"Nancy," Bess began, obviously troubled. "What if Brenda didn't make up that letter? It sounded real to me, and—well, she could really do something to make things worse for that woman."

"That's a pretty scary thought," Nancy agreed. "But think about it. It just seems like too much of a coincidence that you were teasing Brenda about how dull her column was only yesterday, and today—"

She never got to finish her sentence because at that moment, she heard a man cry, "Look out!"

Nancy spun, instantly alert. About fifty yards away Brenda was standing by the metal scaffolding in the middle of the main concourse. She was staring up, her face pale as death. She seemed to be frozen with fear.

A massive wooden beam had apparently slid off the workmen's platform, four stories above —and was hurtling straight at Brenda!

Chapter

Four

BRENDA!" NANCY SHOUTED. She sprinted forward, but as she moved, she knew she didn't have a chance of getting to Brenda before the beam struck.

Nancy's voice must have awakened Brenda from her trance, though. Suddenly the young reporter gave a shrill scream and threw herself backward. A split second later the beam crashed down with a deafening clatter and bounced on the marble floor—right where she had been standing.

Nancy raced to Brenda's side. "Are you all right?" she asked breathlessly.

Brenda was unable to speak. She only nodded, her teeth chattering and her dark eyes round as two buttons. Nancy followed Brenda's horrified gaze to the beam, and her breath caught in her throat. The four-inch-thick plank was cracked along its entire length from the fall. There was no way Brenda would have survived being struck by it!

"I saw it," Nancy heard someone say. She raised her eyes to see a woman in a baker's cap and apron. "I was standing right over there behind the counter, and I saw the whole thing." The woman shook a finger at Brenda. "You're lucky to be alive!"

Bess and George had rushed over right behind Nancy, and a few other people were coming over to see what was wrong. Bess put an arm around Brenda, who looked as if she might faint.

"Whew," George said softly to Nancy, glancing at the fallen beam. "If that thing had hit Brenda . . ."

Nancy nodded gravely. "It was close," she said. Her gaze traveled up the sides of the scaffold to the platform at the top. It appeared to be deserted. Nancy checked her watch. One o'clock—the workers were probably at lunch.

"If there's no one up there, how did the beam fall?" she wondered aloud.

Nancy heard Brenda draw in her breath sharply. Looking over, she saw two spots of color flaming in Brenda's pale cheeks.

"You don't look well," George told her.

"Maybe I should call an ambulance," the woman from the bakery offered.

"An ambulance?" Brenda's voice was shaky,

but she managed a scornful laugh. "I think you'd better call the police."

Bess frowned. "Police?" she said. "Surely for an accident like this—"

"Accident!" Brenda shrieked, twisting away from Bess. "You *would* think it was an accident. Well, it wasn't, let me tell you. Someone just tried to kill me!"

"What?" Nancy's jaw dropped. "Brenda, what are you saying?"

The reporter's dark eyes glittered. "Isn't it obvious?" she retorted. "I'm talking about my column. Someone clearly doesn't want me to be in touch with that woman. The person must know I'm about to uncover the truth!"

"How do you figure that? Did you see someone up there?" Nancy asked dubiously.

"No," Brenda said with an impatient flick of her fingers. "I was just minding my own business and—wham!"

"How could anyone have dropped that beam on you?" Nancy asked. "There was no one up there to drop it."

"Exactly," said Brenda triumphantly. "The perfect alibi—or so the murderer thinks." She pointed dramatically at the platform. "That board should be dusted for fingerprints. I want to talk to the mall manager, and then I want to talk to the police. This was a deliberate attempt on my life, and I want them to do something about it."

Nancy suppressed a groan. Leaning close to

Bess and George, she whispered, "I think what we're seeing here is an attempt to get some free publicity for Brenda's column."

"You mean she's making up all that stuff about someone wanting to kill her?" Bess demanded, sounding outraged.

Nodding, Nancy said, "I think so. I'm going to ask around, but I doubt anyone saw anything—there probably wasn't anything suspicious to see."

Sure enough, none of the people the girls questioned had noticed anything unusual. Nancy even tracked down some of the construction workers and talked to the manager. By the time the police arrived and Brenda began her story again, Nancy was completely fed up.

"Come on, let's get out of here," she said to Bess and George.

The three girls were turning to leave when Nancy's eye was caught by an amazingly good-looking young man in the crowd around Brenda. The guy was well over six feet tall, with a mane of unruly blond hair and piercing green eyes. He was staring at Brenda as if he were seeing a ghost.

Nancy stopped short. What's the matter with that guy? she wondered with a prickle of unease.

Almost as if he sensed her gaze, the guy turned and stared directly at Nancy. A deep flush spread over his tanned face. He quickly averted his eyes and hurried away, pushing through the crowd.

"Boy, this is my week for spotting faces in the crowd," Nancy mumbled. She gestured with her head at the young man, who was just turning for a last look at Brenda. "Now, *he* looks like a guy with a guilty conscience."

"He just looks gorgeous to me," Bess said appreciatively. "If you want to follow him, Nan, I'm game."

Nancy and George broke into a laugh. "Thanks. I'm sure you're offering only out of the goodness of your heart," Nancy teased.

"What about David Park?" George asked. "Yesterday he was your idea of a total dream."

Bess's blue eyes sparkled with mischief as she retorted, "So I have a lot of dreams. Come on, let's go home and get ready for tonight."

"Wow, you look fantastic!" Ned exclaimed when he arrived at the Drews' that evening. His brown eyes held a warm glow of admiration.

Nancy pirouetted in front of him. The silky skirt of her dress flared out around her slender legs in a riot of bright, tropical colors. "Like it?"

"I love it," Ned said, pulling her into his arms for a kiss. "I just hope Dave and Jonathan aren't as dazzled as I am. After all, they're supposed to be with Bess and George. So how was your day?"

"Very weird." Nancy told him about the incident with Brenda at the mall. "So now she's going around saying someone is trying to kill her," she concluded. "Can you believe it?"

Ned shrugged. "Maybe someone *is* trying to kill her."

"I don't think so," she said. "I mean, I actually asked around, just in case, but no one saw anything."

"Are you sure?" Ned asked, his eyes gleaming mischievously. "Someone might want revenge for the advice Brenda gave in her column."

"Hey, I never thought of that," Nancy said, giggling. "You could be right."

The front bell rang, and Nancy opened the door to let Bess and George in. Bess looked terrific in her new, thigh-length dusky pink blouse with a pair of white leggings underneath. George wore a black sleeveless blouse and a black miniskirt with chunky gold earrings.

"Wow! You guys are really dressed to kill," Ned said when he saw them. "Those guys don't stand a chance!"

Jonathan and David arrived soon after. Nancy had already started the coals, and before long the six were sitting on the back porch, their plates piled high with food.

"Well, the tornadoes seem to have held off,"

David commented as he took a second drumstick from the platter on the table.

"Keep your fingers crossed," Bess said. She spooned more potato salad onto David's plate and flashed him a dazzling smile.

Nancy peeked discreetly at George and Jonathan, who were sitting a little apart. George leaned forward, her dark eyes sparkling as she nodded agreement to something Jonathan was saying.

"Pretty good matchmaking, Drew," Ned whispered in her ear.

"I am the best. Aren't I?" Nancy whispered back.

The sun was just setting when they headed over to the lake. Nancy and Ned drove in his green Chevy, while the others went in David's car.

"We've still got about forty-five minutes before Ice Planet starts playing," Jonathan said after they met up in the parking lot. "Just enough time to get a soda and find a spot to sit."

They had almost reached the refreshment stand when Nancy felt a tug on her arm. "Hey, there's Brenda," Bess said. "She doesn't seem to be with anyone—do you think she came alone?"

Nancy followed Bess's gaze over to where Brenda was standing by herself. She looked very pretty in a white jumpsuit, but she seemed to be very uncomfortable.

"Seems that way. She looks lonely," Nancy said. Sighing, she added, "I'll probably regret this, but I'm going to ask her to join us."

Threading her way through the crowd of fans, Nancy tapped Brenda on the shoulder. "Hi," she said. "Have you recovered from this afternoon?"

"Oh—hi." Brenda seemed taken aback. "Yes, I'm fine."

"Did the police find any prints on that beam or on the scaffolding?" Nancy asked politely.

Brenda flushed. "No," she admitted.

Nancy just nodded. Brenda already looked embarrassed about the fuss she had made at the mall. It would be mean to rub her nose in it, though, so all Nancy said was, "I'm here with a bunch of people. Do you want to join us?"

Brenda was obviously torn between suspicion and eagerness. "Well, maybe for a little while," she said at last, making it sound as if she were doing Nancy a big favor.

The reporter followed Nancy back to Ned and the others, but it seemed to Nancy that she was distracted. Brenda hardly joined in the conversation, and she kept peering around at the crowd. Finally she murmured an excuse and wandered away, heading closer to the open-air stage.

"Was it my perfume?" George joked, nodding her head after Brenda.

"Oh, well, we tried," Nancy said, shrugging.

Just then she stiffened. "Look!" she cried, gripping George's arm. "It's the guy I saw at the mall this afternoon."

"The one Bess thought was cute?" George asked.

Nancy nodded distractedly, her eyes still on the tall stranger. He seemed to be strolling aimlessly—but Nancy noticed that his circular path was taking him closer and closer to Brenda Carlton.

Now, why is he following Brenda? Nancy asked herself. She didn't like what she was thinking, but she couldn't avoid the thought. Brenda had already had one narrow escape that day—and the tall stranger had been there when it happened.

It seemed farfetched, but what if this guy was responsible? Was it possible that he was planning to cause *another* "accident"?

Chapter

Five

IN A FLASH Nancy made up her mind. It would be better to make a fool of herself and be wrong than to let something terrible happen to Brenda.

"I'll be right back," she said over her shoulder to the others. Then, without waiting for an answer, she strode purposefully after the tall blond guy.

Within seconds she was in the thick of the crowd that was drifting toward the stage. The sun had set, and with only the last vestiges of daylight to help her, Nancy was having a hard time keeping sight of her quarry. Then, to make things worse, a big, beefy guy in a tank top stepped in front of her, blocking her view completely.

"Excuse me, please," she said, but he didn't seem to hear her. "Uh—excuse me," she said again, in a louder voice. "Could I get by?"

"Huh?" The guy turned and broke into a wide smile as he saw Nancy. "Hey, what's your hurry, Red? You here alone?" he asked.

Nancy frowned and tried to get around him, but he moved to block her way. "My name's Al," he said. "You're cute."

Nancy could hardly contain her impatience. "My name is Nancy," she told him. "I'm in a real hurry. And I'm here with my boyfriend. His name is Ned, but most people just call him Mad Dog."

Al's mouth fell open as he stepped aside.

Nancy hurried on, but to her dismay she'd lost sight of the tall, blond guy. "Oh, no!" she muttered. He probably wasn't up to anything, she reminded herself. But what if she was wrong?

Maybe I should look for Brenda instead, Nancy reasoned. In that white jumpsuit she shouldn't be hard to spot.

Nancy pushed her way closer to the stage, her eyes darting over the growing crowd. The platform had been set up at one end of a grassy lawn enclosed by a split-rail fence and rimmed by a line of towering oak trees. The whole thing was about a hundred yards from the lakeshore. Nancy was almost to the fence when she spotted Brenda, standing alone by the gate. The reporter looked at her wristwatch once, then once again.

At almost the same instant Nancy's eye caught a flash of movement in the trees. A quick glance was enough to give her a good idea of who was lurking among the old oaks. She circled around to the side, her heart pounding.

She wasn't mistaken. The tall, blond stranger stood in the shadow of a massive tree, his hair a bright golden patch in the deepening evening gloom. The guy was definitely studying Brenda. If his intentions were good, why would he be hiding behind a tree?

I guess I might as well be direct, Nancy thought. Stepping quietly up behind the guy, she cleared her throat, causing the stranger to whirl around. He gaped at Nancy, his green eyes wide with alarm.

At his first move Nancy had tensed, ready to defend herself if necessary. Now she relaxed, but only slightly. He doesn't *look* dangerous, she thought. But she knew that didn't mean much—she had met plenty of criminals who had looked as harmless as this guy.

"Excuse me, but I saw you over here in the trees, and I thought you might be lost or something," she said. "Can I help you?"

"Oh, uh, thanks, th-that's very nice of you," the guy stammered. "The fact is, I'm new in town. Well, sort of new—that is, I'm not here permanently. I'm a college student. I'm just here for the summer, staying with my aunt and uncle." He stopped talking abruptly, gave a nervous laugh, and held out his hand. "My name's Rick Waterston."

He's babbling, Nancy thought. What's he so nervous about? She decided to come right out and ask him what he was up to.

"I'm Nancy Drew," she said in a firm, matter-of-fact voice. "I saw you at the mall this afternoon, and you seemed very interested in my friend over there—" She gestured toward Brenda, who was still by the fence gate. "Or at least in the near-accident she had just had. And tonight I saw you following her. I'd like to know why."

Rick's eyes sharpened with interest. "You know her?" he asked quickly. "That's Brenda Carlton, isn't it?"

Folding her arms across her chest, Nancy stared at Rick and asked, "Why do you want to know?"

Rick hesitated for a moment and stared at the ground. "This is going to sound really weird," he began.

"Try me," Nancy offered.

"I need to talk to Brenda," Rick said. "When I saw her this afternoon at the mall, I thought I recognized her. I tried to talk to her there, only then that beam nearly fell on her, and with all the excitement I didn't have a chance. So I left a message at the newspaper she writes a column for and asked her to meet me."

41

THE NANCY DREW FILES

"What do you want to talk to her about?" Nancy pressed.

Rick hesitated again, raking a hand through his thick blond hair. "It's her column," he said at last. "See, there was this letter in it this morning, and my aunt and uncle—well, they haven't been getting along very well lately, and in the last couple of weeks I've noticed some weird things. . . ." Rick trailed off.

Nancy couldn't believe what she was hearing. "Wait a minute. Are you saying your aunt—" she began, but she was interrupted by a shout.

"Nan! There you are. I've been looking everywhere for you."

It was Ned. "Oh, hi," she greeted him distractedly, then introduced him to Rick.

"Nice to meet you," Ned said. He turned back to Nancy. "What's with the disappearing act? The concert's about to start."

Nancy glanced quickly at Rick. "I, uh—I needed to talk to Rick," she said. "He was just telling me something very interesting about his aunt and uncle." Speaking directly to Rick, she added, "I'd like to hear the rest of your story."

But Ned's presence seemed to have put a damper on Rick's willingness to talk. "Oh, it's nothing—it's dumb," he mumbled. "Look, I've got to be going. It was nice meeting both of you."

"Wait," Nancy said. But Rick was already

gone, hurrying along with the crowd that was settling in on the lawn in front of the stage.

Ned looked at her questioningly. "What was that all about?"

"I'm not sure," Nancy said thoughtfully. She told Ned about seeing Rick at the mall, spotting him following Brenda, and then his story about Brenda's column. "But the guy just clammed up the minute you came along," she finished. "I wonder if he was really trying to tell me he thinks his aunt wrote that letter to Brenda?"

Ned turned as the sound of clapping and whistling broke out. "Well, let's not talk about it now. Ice Planet must be getting ready to come onstage. Come on." He grabbed Nancy's hand and pulled her toward the stage. "The others went ahead to scout out a good spot for us, but if we don't get a move on, we'll never find them."

"Okay, okay," Nancy said, hurrying to keep up with him. As they entered the grassy enclosure and picked their way through the crowd, she craned her neck trying to spot Rick or Brenda, but neither was in sight.

The band launched into its first number, just as Ned and Nancy found the blanket their friends had spread out on the grass. Bess scooted over to make room on the blanket for Nancy and Ned.

Ice Planet was one of Nancy's favorite groups, and she began bobbing her head in time to the music. Even so, her thoughts kept returning to what Rick had started to tell her.

Was there really a woman in River Heights who was afraid her husband was trying to kill her? Did that person really try to kill Brenda? Unless Rick had made up what he'd told Nancy—and she didn't know why he would— it was beginning to look as if maybe Brenda *hadn't* made up that letter in her column.

I've got to find out the truth, Nancy thought, because if this woman does exist, then she needs help. And Brenda is putting both herself and the woman in even more danger by publishing those letters and telling the letter writer not to do anything.

"Hey, Nancy, wake up," George scolded. "The concert's over."

"Huh?" Nancy said, blinking. "That was kind of short, wasn't it?"

"They played for over an hour," George informed her, giving her a quizzical look. "They even did that great long version of 'Frozen Out.' Weren't you listening?"

"I guess I was a little bit out of it," Nancy admitted sheepishly.

"Uh-oh," said Bess, leaning around David's shoulder. "I smell a mystery."

Nancy wasn't sure there *was* a mystery, but she wanted to find out if there was before anyone got hurt.

As they were walking back toward the parking lot, Nancy kept an eye out for Rick. They were almost back to Ned's car when she finally spotted him. He was standing a few yards away, by a parked van—and he was talking to Brenda.

Nancy paused to take in the scene. Rick was leaning forward, an intent expression on his face as he spoke. Brenda, her back against the van, was gazing up into his eyes with an intimate smile. As Nancy watched, Brenda placed her hand on Rick's arm.

That's funny, Nancy thought, her eyes narrowing. Rick had led her to think he'd never met Brenda—but that hardly looked like a conversation between two people who didn't know each other.

Nancy knew Brenda well enough to suspect the reporter would stretch the truth if it suited her. She didn't know anything at all about Rick, but she was beginning to get the feeling he hadn't been totally honest with her, either. In any case, Nancy was increasingly sure of one thing—both Rick and Brenda had something to hide.

Chapter
Six

Nancy frowned at the couple. She had to find out once and for all if there really was a murder plot in the planning stage, or if Brenda and Rick were somehow in cahoots and making the whole thing up. She didn't know why Rick would get involved, but there was only one way to find out.

Twining her arm around Ned's waist, Nancy nodded in Rick and Brenda's direction and asked, "Why don't we walk over this way, Ned? I want to check something out."

Ned gave her a puzzled glance but agreed.

After saying good night to the others, Nancy and Ned strolled over to where Rick and Brenda were. Nancy leaned her head on Ned's shoulder, her eyes half-closed, a dreamy smile on her face. But her ears were wide open, straining to catch Brenda and Rick's low-pitched conversation.

"I wish I could, but I can't give you a ride," Brenda was saying. "Daddy is sending his driver to pick me up, and the guy is under orders to take me straight home. Daddy's worried about me, after what happened at the mall today."

Rick's reply was too quiet for Nancy to hear, but apparently it pleased Brenda. She giggled. "That's so sweet of you," she cooed.

"Uh-oh," Ned whispered. "Rick really seems to be fooled by Brenda's sweet act."

"Shh!" Nancy whispered back, stifling a laugh. "You're ruining my concentration."

Just then a long, sleek silver car pulled up beside Brenda.

"Here's my ride," Brenda said to Rick. Her voice sounded genuinely regretful, Nancy thought. "I guess I'd better say good night."

"Okay." Rick sounded hesitant. "Would you have lunch with me tomorrow?" he asked at last. "That is, if you're up to it."

Nancy sneaked a look at Brenda from under her lashes. Brenda's dark eyes were shining. "I'd love to," she said. "Call me at the paper in the morning. *Ciao!*"

With that she climbed into the back seat of the silver car. Before Brenda closed the car door, she caught Nancy's eye, and Nancy saw triumph in the look. Then the door closed, and the big sedan surged away.

Ned looked at Nancy. *"Ciao?"* he echoed in a dubious tone.

"Leave it to Brenda," Nancy said with a sigh of disappointment. She hadn't learned anything at all yet, though the look Brenda had given her made Nancy think *something* was up.

"Hey, look who's coming toward us," she murmured a moment later.

It was Rick. He approached them with a smile. "Hi," he said. "I'm glad to see a couple of familiar faces."

Nancy raised her eyebrows. It was a bit of a stretch to call her and Ned familiar.

"I was wondering," Rick went on smoothly. "I took a cab here tonight, and Brenda tells me it's hard to get a cab to come out here this late. Would it be too much trouble to give me a lift back to town?"

Nancy was puzzled. Why was he being so friendly now, when before he'd practically run away from them? She couldn't help wondering if this was part of some plan he and Brenda had hatched. What was his game?

Nancy was glad when Ned said, "Sure, no problem." He gestured down the row of cars to their right. "My Chevy's parked right over there."

Now, at least, she'd have a chance to dig deeper into Rick's story about his aunt being in danger. "So, Rick, you were telling me about your aunt and uncle before," Nancy said casually as the three of them walked to Ned's car.

"Oh, right," Rick said. "Listen, forget about it. I shouldn't have been going on about their problems—it's really none of my business."

"You know, Nancy is a detective," Ned put in. They reached his car, and he unlocked it. "If you're really worried, talk to her. She can get to the bottom of anything."

"A detective? No kidding!" Rick exclaimed. From the too-bright tone of his voice, Nancy was almost positive Ned's comment wasn't news to him.

"Maybe you *can* help me," Rick said. He gave her a disarming grin. "Do you really want to hear my story?"

Nancy climbed into the passenger's seat. "Definitely," she said. He sounded as if he had rehearsed every word. This ought to be good! Nancy told herself.

Rick climbed into the back seat, and Ned slid in behind the wheel. A moment later he was pulling into the stream of traffic leaving the concert.

"I've always been close to my aunt," Rick began, leaning forward and resting his arms on the back of Nancy's bucket seat. "She's my godmother, too, and—well, several months ago she invited me to spend the summer with her and her new husband. But when I got here, he seemed very put out about my being here."

"You said he's your aunt's new husband?" Ned asked, glancing at Rick in the rearview mirror. "If they're newlyweds, maybe he just wants time to be alone with his bride."

Rick shook his head. "They're not newly-weds. I meant to say he's her *second* husband. They've been married over a year. No, he just doesn't want me around. I even heard them arguing about it one morning, when they thought I was still in bed. At one point Bi—my uncle said, 'Why did Rick have to come *now?*'"

Nancy was sure Rick had been about to say his uncle's name before he stopped himself. Why wouldn't he want her to know who his uncle was? Aloud, she asked, "What did your aunt say?"

"She didn't say anything," Rick answered. "She just burst into tears. She's been doing that a lot lately. And that's not like my aunt. She's usually a really fun-loving type."

"Mmm. Go on," Nancy prompted.

"Well, this morning we were having break-fast. My uncle had already left for work. My aunt was reading *Today's Times,* and suddenly she let out a funny little noise. She had turned totally white and appeared to be really shaken up." Rick blew out his breath. "I asked her what was wrong, but she wouldn't give me a straight answer. She gave me some line about how she'd been reading about tornadoes and how much they scared her. But I knew she was lying, because *I* had the news section. She was reading Lifestyles."

"So later you checked out the Lifestyles section, and you saw the letter in Brenda's advice column from the woman who thinks her husband is trying to kill her," Nancy guessed.

Inwardly, she was thinking, Oh, you're good, Brenda. You actually convinced this guy to back up your claim about someone being in trouble. She still couldn't think of why Rick would go along with the story, though. Maybe he just had a crush on Brenda.

"Right," Rick was saying. "And I made a connection—" He broke off abruptly. "Wait, let me backtrack." His voice grew sober. "See, I wouldn't have thought anything about that letter, except that just yesterday my aunt was in a car accident. And the letter had something in it about the husband sabotaging the wife's car."

"But didn't the woman who wrote the letter say that she hasn't driven her car since she saw her husband tampering with it?" Ned pointed out, wheeling his Chevy into a right turn.

Rick shrugged and sat back. "Sure, but so what? That letter was probably written a few days ago. The accident was yesterday. Maybe something made her change her mind about driving.

"I wanted to see the letter Brenda got," Rick continued. "I called the newspaper office this

morning, and the receptionist told me Brenda
had just left for the mall, so I went there to find
her," Rick said. His voice grew sheepish. "The
hardest part was getting up the nerve to ap-
proach her. A girl as gorgeous as Brenda—
well, I was afraid she wouldn't even give me
the time of day."

In the driver's seat Ned turned and raised
his eyebrows at Nancy. Rick sure was laying it
on thick. Brenda must have loved coaching
him on this part of their story!

Rick leaned forward again. "I recognized
Brenda from her picture in the paper. I was
sort of following her when she stopped to talk
to you, Nancy. Then the next thing I knew, she
was practically killed by that beam, and
Brenda was saying someone did it on purpose
because of her column." He gave a little laugh.
"Let me tell you, that really shook me up."

Turning in the front seat to look at Rick
Nancy commented, "Well, you and Brenda
seemed to hit it off tonight. Did she show you
the letter?"

"Not yet," Rick admitted. "She has good
reasons not to—she said it would be a viola-
tion of the writer's privacy, and it would
compromise freedom of the press. But I'm still
trying."

Nancy had to admit that Rick and Brenda
had thought of all the angles. But it was
suspicious that he hadn't actually mentioned
names. "Rick, if you don't mind my asking,"

Nancy said, "don't you think you should go to the police with this information? What's your aunt's name, anyway?"

"Oh, you wouldn't know her," he said in a rush. Rick seemed immensely relieved when Ned broke into the conversation.

"Excuse me, Rick," said Ned. "Where should I drop you off?"

"The corner of Grange and Spruce," Rick said.

"It's no problem for us to take you right to your aunt's house," Ned protested.

Rick seemed a bit flustered. "No—no, really, it's not necessary. Grange and Spruce is just fine. Really."

"Okay," Ned agreed, shrugging. "Whatever."

A moment later, following Rick's directions, Ned pulled over at the intersection of Grange and Spruce, and Rick climbed out of the back seat. After thanking Nancy and Ned, he walked off into the darkness.

"Hmm," Nancy mumbled as she gazed around. "Recognize this neighborhood, Ned?"

He peered through the windshield to where the headlights illuminated a big stone house. "Looks pretty ritzy."

"It is," Nancy informed him. "And it just so happens Brenda Carlton's house is only about a block away."

Ned whistled. "Hey. Are you saying Rick is on his way to see Brenda right now?"

"I wouldn't be surprised," Nancy said. She crossed her arms and frowned out into the night. "You know what? I think Brenda is using this guy Rick as part of some kind of campaign to convince the world—or me, at least—that the letter in this morning's column was serious."

"You mean he's lying about his aunt?"

"I think so," Nancy said uncertainly. Shrugging, she added, "Rick seems to have a crush on Brenda. She could be using that to get him to feed us this whole story. It's—"

Nancy was interrupted by a shout, followed by the echoing sound of rapid footsteps on pavement. Peering out her window, she saw a muscular man of medium height dash through the beams of the headlights. Close on his heels was a taller figure.

"It's Rick!" Nancy exclaimed, recognizing the second figure.

The shorter man was faster than Rick. He raced forward and snapped his head back briefly to check out his pursuer.

Nancy gasped when she saw his face. It was the man she'd seen the day of the car accident—the guy with the mismatched eyes!

Chapter

Seven

IN A MOMENT he was gone, swallowed up in the darkness of the tree-lined street. Rick continued to tear after him.

"Ned, I've seen that guy before!" Nancy cried, jumping out of the car. "He was in the mall parking lot the day Brenda had her accident."

Ned climbed out of the car, too, and came around to stand by Nancy. "So what does that mean?" he asked, looking baffled.

Just then Rick reappeared and crossed the street toward Ned's car. He was frowning, and his face was shiny with sweat. "I lost him," he panted. Bracing his hands against the hood of the car, he bent over, inhaling deeply.

"Rick, what happened?" Nancy asked urgently.

"I saw that guy prowling around my aunt and uncle's house," Rick replied. He straightened up indignantly. "I'd better go call the cops."

Nancy laid a hand on Rick's arm as he was turning to go. "Did you get a good look at him?" she asked. "The police will need a description."

"I only saw him from the back," Rick said, shaking his head.

"Well, I saw him," Nancy told him. "He shouldn't be too hard to spot—he's unusual looking. He has one blue eye and one brown eye."

At her last words Rick blinked, and a wary expression spread over his face. Nancy had the distinct impression that her description rang a bell with Rick. "Do you know anyone like that?" she asked him.

"Uh—no," Rick said quickly.

Why was he lying? "Maybe I should be there when you talk to the police," Nancy pressed. "I seem to be the only witness who actually saw the man's face."

"I don't want to put you out. In fact, maybe I shouldn't go to the police. The guy is probably long gone by now, and it would only scare my aunt if she knew he'd been around." Rick had suddenly become nervous and in a hurry to leave. "Well, good night and thanks again."

Back in the car Ned turned to Nancy. "What do you think made him change his mind about going to the police?" he asked. "That was weird."

"I thought so, too," Nancy agreed. "He seemed to recognize the man's description, but he sure wasn't about to tell us who it was."

Whatever Ned was about to say was interrupted by a tremendous yawn. "I'm beat. I'd better get you home," he said. "Why is it that so many of my dates with you turn into major adventures?"

"I just like to keep you on your toes, Nickerson," Nancy retorted playfully.

As they drove the short distance to the Drews' house, questions whirled dizzily in Nancy's mind. Who was the man with the different-colored eyes? Did Rick really have an aunt? And if so, who was she? Was her husband trying to kill her? Had she really written a letter to Brenda's column? Or were Rick and Brenda trying to pull a hoax?

Suddenly Nancy found herself yawning, too. I'll get a good night's rest, she thought to herself, and tomorrow I'll start digging out the real story behind the letter in Brenda's column!

Nancy glanced out the window of her second-floor bedroom, toweling her hair dry after her morning shower. Heat was already rising in shimmering waves from the shingles of the porch roof. It was going to be another scorcher.

After putting on a pair of shorts and a maroon T-shirt, she went out to her Mustang and drove to pick up a copy of *Today's Times*. When she returned, her father was seated in the dining room, eating a breakfast of French toast, juice, and coffee. He greeted Nancy with a smile that crinkled the corners of his dark eyes.

In contrast to Nancy's reddish hair, Carson Drew's was dark brown, though it was now flecked with silver at his temples. His face was square, while Nancy's was a delicate oval. But both father and daughter had the same straight nose—and the same gleam of intelligence and determination in their eyes.

"Morning, Dad," Nancy said cheerfully, setting the paper on the table as she sat down. "I hope you saved me some breakfast."

"There's a stack of French toast in the warming dish," Carson answered, pointing to a covered dish on the table. "And there's bacon and melon slices. Hannah's out doing errands, but she made sure we wouldn't starve."

Nancy helped herself. "You must be busy— you've been at the office late a lot this week."

"I've been swamped." Looking over his coffee cup at her, Carson said, "As a matter of fact, I have to ask a favor. I need a cashier's check from my bank, but I can't get there today—I've got meetings until six o'clock tonight. Would you mind going for me?"

Nancy shook her head. "No problem."

"Thanks." Carson pushed his chair back and stood up. "I've got to get going. I'll call you from the office and let you know the exact sum."

Nancy blew him a kiss. Then she opened her copy of *Today's Times* and turned to Brenda's column.

"Wow," she muttered. Brenda hadn't printed any letters that day. Instead, the entire column was a dramatic plea to the woman who was afraid her husband was trying to murder her.

"Please contact me!" the column trumpeted in big letters. "You can't survive this terrible crisis alone. You need the help of a sensitive, intelligent, resourceful person. I am that person, but you have to come to me."

"Oh, brother," Nancy muttered out loud. Brenda was really coming on strong.

Setting the paper back down on the table, Nancy thought through her plans for that day. After she went to the bank, she'd go to the paper to see if she could get her hands on the letter that woman had supposedly written. It was definitely time to get to the bottom of this.

"You'll have to get an approval from the bank manager, miss." The teller raised her eyebrows apologetically at Nancy. "I'm not authorized to dispense that kind of cash."

Letting out a sigh, Nancy thanked the teller

and headed for the manager's office. The office door was open, and Nancy could see a stocky man with gray hair cut short in military style behind the desk.

It was just her luck that he was busy with another customer. She'd already waited in line for twenty minutes, but she had no choice but to take a seat and wait some more.

After a few minutes she began to get impatient. The bank manager didn't seem to be in any great hurry. In fact, he and his customer seemed to be swapping war stories!

"And frankly, Bill, I was *scared,*" the customer was saying. "But I crawled on my belly until I reached the arsenal, and then I pulled out my last grenade and chucked it in. And then I ran. Brother, those were some fireworks!"

The bank manager chuckled. "I'll bet. Say, did I ever tell you about the time I blew up a convoy of enemy supply trucks in a tunnel?"

Ugh, what a gruesome conversation! Nancy shifted uncomfortably on the hard plastic seat outside the office.

"It was so simple, it was beautiful," the manager declared. "The tunnel had been sealed at one end by a rock slide. It was a protected location, in the heart of a mountain —impossible to bomb, and so deep in enemy territory they never thought they'd have to worry about security."

Nancy was trying not to get annoyed. She'd

heard of good customer relations, but this was carrying it a bit far.

"I parachuted in at night," the manager was saying, "and slipped into the tunnel before the convoy arrived. I planted a bottle of ether at the sealed end. Then I went to the open end, lit a candle, and left. A few hours later the ether fumes reached the candle flame, and— boom!"

Nancy began tapping her foot against the carpeted floor, letting her gaze roam around the manager's office. Suddenly she sat up straighter in her chair as she read the nameplate on his desk. William A. Keating.

Wait a second— Could he be related to Maggie Keating, the woman who'd crashed into Brenda at the mall? It wasn't a very common name; it made sense that they could be related.

Then another idea hit Nancy. The previous night Rick had cut himself off in the middle of saying his uncle's name. He'd said "Bi—" and then changed it to "my uncle." What if he had been about to say "Bill"? As in Bill *Keating?*

Nancy's eyes widened. If Mr. Keating was Rick's uncle, and Mrs. Keating was Rick's aunt, and she had had a car accident . . .

Could it be that Rick's story was true and the letter was genuine? Could Maggie Keating have written it? Could the bank manager be a killer?

"Can I help you?"

Nancy came out of her thoughts with a start to see Mr. Keating in the doorway, beckoning to her. His other customer had gone.

Nancy managed a smile. "Sure." She handed him her withdrawal slip and asked him to approve it.

Just then the speaker phone on Keating's desk buzzed.

"Excuse me." Leaning over the intercom speaker, he said, "Yes?"

"Mr. Keating, the auditors want to move the inspection up to next Monday. Will that be all right with you?" inquired a tinny voice.

"Monday? What was wrong with Wednesday?" Keating asked sharply.

"I don't know, sir," the voice replied.

Keating frowned. "All right, fine. Make it Monday." The intercom clicked off.

Keating looked up at Nancy. "Excuse the interruption," he said, smiling. He scrawled his initials on the slip and handed it to her. "There you are, young lady. Have a nice afternoon."

"Thanks," Nancy told him. "You, too."

Nancy could barely bring herself to wait for the teller to make out the cashier's check. When she finally got it, she drove it over to her father's law firm. He was between meetings, so she took it into his office herself.

"Thanks," her father said when she handed him the draft. "Did you have any trouble?"

"Not really, but I had to get an approval from Mr. Keating, the bank manager." Nancy sank into a red leather chair by her father's desk. "Dad, what do you know about him?"

"Who? Keating?" Carson asked, sounding surprised. "Not much. Why?"

Nancy briefly told him all that had been happening the past few days, and about the possible connection she'd just made between the Keatings and the letters in Brenda's column.

"I'd hate to think Maggie could be in any trouble," Carson said when Nancy had finished, a frown creasing his forehead. "She's a fine person, used to be married to a lawyer I knew, Wilford Trout. He passed away about five years ago, and last year Maggie married Keating."

Leveling a serious look at his daughter, Carson went on. "I have to admit I don't know much about Bill. He hasn't been in town long—the bank brought him in from Chicago several years ago.

"I hear he's a bit of a high roller, though. Some of the bank's directors feel his investment policies are risky." He shrugged. "That's all I know."

"All?" Nancy cried. "Dad, you're amazing!" Thinking out loud, she added, "I doubt Mr. Keating would want to kill his wife just to get back at her for not being wealthy. So what's his motive?" She drummed her fingers on the chair arm, deep in thought, then snapped up straight and said, "Unless he's going to *get* money by murdering her—insurance money, for instance."

Carson leaned forward. "Nancy, this could be serious. Don't you think it's a matter for the police?"

"So far I'm just guessing, Dad. I'm not even sure Mrs. Keating really is Rick's aunt or that she's the woman who wrote the letter to Brenda." Nancy jumped to her feet. "But I'm definitely going to find out."

Nancy swung her Mustang right onto the street where the Keatings lived and started scanning the numbers for 357, the address she'd found in the phone book. She located it just down the street from the corner where she and Ned had dropped Rick off after the concert the night before.

Well, at least Rick wasn't lying about where his aunt lives—if Mrs. Keating really is his aunt, Nancy reminded herself.

At first Nancy saw only the long, sloping lawn edged with tall, leafy trees. It wasn't until after she turned into the driveway that the house came into view. Set back from the street, it was large and ornately Victorian, with round turrets, lots of gingerbread woodwork, and a sloping roof over the porch.

Nancy didn't see any cars in the driveway, but then Mrs. Keating's sedan was probably in the shop after her accident with Brenda. After braking her own car to a stop, Nancy got out, went to the front door, and rang the bell.

When the door opened, Nancy saw that Mrs. Keating still appeared to be distraught and that there were dark circles under her eyes.

"Mrs. Keating," Nancy began, "you may not remember me, but I was at the mall when you had your accident the day before yesterday. I'm Nancy Drew."

"Yes, of course," Mrs. Keating said, without smiling. She reached up with one hand and nervously patted her ash blond hair. "Is there some problem?"

Nancy wanted to clear one thing up right away. "I'm a friend of your nephew's—"

Mrs. Keating's expression brightened slightly as she said, "Rick? Well, I'm afraid he's not here at the moment. Now, if you'll excuse me—"

She began to close the door, but Nancy stuck out her hand to hold it open. "Mrs. Keating, please. I'd like to talk to you about the accident. Rick seemed very worried, and I—"

"Please! There's nothing to say." Mrs. Keating was visibly shaken by Nancy's insistence, but then slowly she got her feelings under control. "I'm sorry," she went on in a calmer voice, "but I'm late for an appointment. Now, goodbye." With that she closed the door in Nancy's face.

Shaking her head, Nancy walked back to her car. Whatever Mrs. Keating was nervous about, she wasn't about to fill Nancy in on it. So now what?

After driving home, Nancy phoned Ned at work.

"Hi, it's me," she said into the receiver when he answered. "Will you do me a big favor?"

"If I can," Ned answered. "What's up?"

"I need information on someone who may be a client of Mutual Life," Nancy told him.

"I can't give you information about policy-holders," Ned protested. "It's confidential. I could get fired for doing that."

"I know, and I hate to ask," Nancy replied. "But this is important." Quickly she explained her idea about Mrs. Keating being the letter writer. "I need to find out what kind of life insurance Mrs. Keating has. If it's enough to kill for . . ."

"Then she's in trouble," Ned finished. "Okay. I'll see what I can find out."

Five minutes later he called her back. "She is one of our clients, all right. I had to go into the mainframe computer files to check out her coverage," he reported. "That's where the big-ticket policies are maintained."

"Big-ticket?" Nancy repeated. "What's that?"

"Any coverage over two hundred thousand

dollars," Ned said. "Mrs. Keating's policy has only been in the big-ticket file for six months."

Nancy felt a rush of anticipation. "What does that mean?" she asked excitedly.

"It means that six months ago, Mrs. Keating's life insurance coverage jumped—to a cool million dollars!"

Chapter

Eight

NANCY TIGHTENED HER GRIP on the receiver. "Ned, are you serious?" she gasped.

"You bet. Mrs. Keating has had a policy with us for almost ten years," he explained in a grim voice. "Her coverage was a hundred thousand dollars—until January. That was when Mr. Keating arranged for them both to receive much more substantial policies."

"Wow," Nancy murmured. She picked up the phone, carried it over to the sofa, and sat down. "I can't believe this. Maybe Brenda has stumbled onto a real case."

"And she's totally botching it up," Ned added. "We've got to do something, Nan."

Nancy thought for a second. "How about this?" she suggested, glancing at her watch. "It's four now. Can you leave work a little early?"

"I guess so," Ned replied after a moment.

"Great. Meet me here at my house. You and I are going to pay a little visit to Brenda." Nancy's brows drew together in a determined frown. "It's time we got a straight story from her."

"On my way, chief," Ned said, then hung up.

Nancy raised her eyes as Hannah bustled into the room. "I thought I heard you in here," the housekeeper said. "I just came in from the garden. My, but it's hot today! Come on into the kitchen and I'll fix us both some iced tea."

"Mmm, sounds good," said Nancy, following Hannah into the kitchen. Still deep in thought, she reached distractedly for two glasses and filled them with ice.

"By the way, Bess called while you were out," Hannah said, pouring tea into the glasses. "She wants you to call her back late tonight. She sounded very excited—said something about a date with someone named David."

"Hmm? Oh, that's nice," Nancy said vaguely.

"Let me guess—you've got a new mystery."

With a start Nancy realized that the house-keeper was peering at her closely. "You're right, Hannah. I guess you know me pretty well."

"I should say so!" Hannah replied firmly.

They sat down at the kitchen table, and Nancy told Hannah about the Keating case. As she was finishing, Ned arrived, flushed and scowling.

"The air conditioning in my old clunker is out," he said. "I'm just about roasted. Let's take your car, Nan."

"Sure," Nancy agreed, grinning as Ned downed in one giant gulp the glass of iced tea she had poured for him. She put both their glasses in the sink, then headed for the front door, calling over her shoulder, "I'll be home for dinner, Hannah."

They drove to the *Today's Times* offices, in downtown River Heights, only to be told by the receptionist that Brenda had left. Ten minutes later Nancy guided her blue Mustang up the Carltons' steep driveway.

"Here we are," Nancy announced. "Finally."

As the house came into view, Ned exclaimed, "Wow! I'd forgotten what a castle this place is."

The Carltons' enormous white house was perched on a knoll overlooking several acres of grounds. Manicured green lawns swept down to a high, well-trimmed hedge. Beyond the hedge a thick belt of trees all but hid the neighboring house, a huge brick mansion.

"It's pretty impressive," Nancy agreed. She steered her car into a gravel turnaround and parked. Then she and Ned got out, went up to the pillared porch, and rang the doorbell. A uniformed maid answered.

"Hi," Nancy said. "We're friends of Brenda's. Is she home?"

"Miss Carlton is out by the pool," the maid replied. "May I tell her who's calling?"

"Oh, don't bother to announce us," Nancy said quickly. "We'd like to surprise her." She didn't want to give Brenda the chance to avoid them.

The maid hesitated briefly but then led them through the house and out a set of glass doors that opened onto a flagstone patio. "Right down those steps," she directed.

Brenda, clad in a white two-piece bathing suit decorated with long fringe, lay on a chaise longue by the kidney-shaped swimming pool. When she saw Nancy and Ned, her expression was anything but welcoming. "What do you want?" she demanded.

"Some answers," Nancy shot back.

"Hey!" a new voice broke in. Nancy turned and was surprised to see Rick Waterston emerging from the bathhouse, wearing a pair of swim trunks. "Hi!" he called, waving. "I didn't know you two were coming over. Did you bring your suits?" he asked.

Although she hadn't expected to see Rick, Nancy was glad for the chance to question them both. "We're just here for a moment," she told him. "May I ask you something?"

"Shoot," Rick replied, grinning easily.

"Why didn't you tell us Maggie Keating is your aunt?"

Rick's smile faded, and he sputtered, "How'd you know—hey! Has something happened to her?"

"Not that I know of," Nancy told him. After a short pause she added, "Not yet, anyway."

"What are you trying to say?" Rick asked.

Taking a deep breath, Nancy explained, "I'm saying that I believe your aunt is in serious danger from her husband. I'm sorry I doubted your story last night." She glanced at Brenda, who wore a look of blank surprise on her face. "But if we work together now, it may not be too late to save your aunt."

"Tell me what to do," Rick said instantly.

"Rick!" Brenda protested, jumping up from her lounge and going over to him. "Didn't I tell you I could handle it?"

"Yeah, but if Aunt Maggie really is in trouble, I'll take all the help I can get." Rick's voice was apologetic but firm.

Brenda opened her mouth to say something, but Rick put his hand gently over it. "Please."

To Nancy's amazement, Brenda subsided.

"Incredible!" Ned murmured. Brenda shot him a dirty look but remained quiet.

Nancy and Ned pulled up deck chairs and sat.

"Rick, why was it such a big deal for you to keep your aunt's identity a secret?" Nancy asked.

With an apologetic glance at Brenda, Rick said, "It was Brenda's idea. I just—"

"You don't have to go sticking your nose in every single case that comes along, Nancy," Brenda said hotly. "We were doing just fine on our own!"

Ignoring Brenda's outburst, Nancy asked Rick, "Can you add anything more to what you told us last night?"

Rick began pacing up and down by the edge of the pool. "Not a lot," he admitted, frowning. "All I have is a bunch of vague suspicions."

Nancy glanced at Brenda, half expecting her to interrupt again, but the reporter just stared sulkily. Turning back to Rick, Nancy urged, "Tell us about your uncle. What's he like?"

"Well," Rick said, pausing to look at her, "to be honest, no one in my family is too crazy about Uncle Bill. He's one of those gung-ho types. He used to be in the army, and he never stops talking about the service and all the incredible missions he was on. I think he probably exaggerates."

Nancy smiled slightly, thinking of the story she'd overheard in the bank earlier that day.

"Is he nice to your aunt?" Ned asked.

"I guess so," Rick replied, shrugging. "My mom thinks he married Aunt Maggie for her money, but I don't know about that. She isn't rich. Her first husband had some family money to start out with, I think, but by the time he died, there wasn't much left. Uncle Wilford spent most of it on racehorses. The Trouts— that's Uncle Wilford's family—are famous for their expensive hobbies, and Aunt Maggie's a pretty big spender herself."

Rick gave a short laugh. "If Uncle Bill did marry her for her money, he must have been pretty disappointed."

I'll bet, Nancy thought.

"That's the thing I don't get," Rick went on. "Why would Uncle Bill want to kill her? If he's after a wife with money, why doesn't he just divorce Aunt Maggie?"

Nancy and Ned exchanged a knowing glance. Clearing his throat, Ned explained about Mr. Keating's increasing the insurance policy on Rick's aunt to a million dollars.

Rick drew in his breath in a shocked gasp. "Oh, no," he murmured, his face a ghostly white.

"We think he's after that million dollars," Nancy added. "But we need some hard evidence. Unless we can prove our suspicions to the authorities, we can't help your aunt." She leaned forward to take in Brenda.

"What are you staring at *me* for?" Brenda demanded hotly.

"You're the one who holds the key to this case," Nancy said. "The letter from Mrs. Keating. You have to show it to us."

Brenda glared. "No way! I can't reveal my

source," she protested. "It would ruin my reputation as a reporter."

"We already guessed who wrote the letter," Ned said angrily. "Besides, a woman's life is more important than your reputation as a reporter, Brenda. That letter is the only solid piece of evidence in this whole case. Without it the police won't even listen to us."

"But the letter was confidential," Brenda objected stubbornly.

"Please," Rick begged. He took Brenda's hands in his and stared into her eyes. "My aunt's life is at stake. I need your help."

Brenda looked torn but remained silent. Gazing at her, Nancy was struck with a sudden thought—one she didn't like at all.

"Brenda, when did you get the letter?" she asked.

Brenda flushed. "Tuesday," she said. "The day I had the accident at the mall."

"Morning or afternoon?" Nancy demanded quickly.

"Morning, I think," Brenda mumbled, looking flustered.

"What did it look like?"

"Wh-what do you mean?" Brenda stammered.

"What did it look like?" Nancy repeated. "Was it handwritten?"

"Yes—I mean no. It was typed."

Aha! That was Brenda's first slip. "How long

was it?" Nancy asked, continuing to grill the reporter.

"I don't remember." Brenda's voice was becoming shrill. "What does it matter? I don't like the third degree, Nancy!"

"You don't?" Nancy asked sharply. "Then show us the letter, Brenda."

"I can't show it to you," Brenda insisted. "I can't. Now, stop bugging me!"

Nancy folded her arms and gave Brenda a piercing look. "I think I know why you can't show it to us," she said.

Brenda glared at her but said nothing.

"You can't show it to us because there *is* no letter," Nancy accused, unable to keep the anger from her voice.

"What—?" Rick said, an expression of shock coming over his face.

Brenda took one look at him and buried her face in her hands. "You're right," she confessed in a muffled voice. "I made the whole thing up!"

Chapter

Nine

FOR A MOMENT Nancy just stared at Brenda. She was furious with the reporter, but what made it even worse was that she herself had ended up buying Brenda's dumb stunt.

"Wait a minute," Rick said, his green eyes bewildered. "You mean you made the letter up? This woman whose husband wants to kill her—she doesn't exist?"

Brenda fiddled nervously with the white fringe on her bathing suit. Without looking up, she nodded.

"And the accident in the mall, with the beam. You said someone was trying to kill you," Rick said. "Were you just making that up, too?"

Brenda nodded again, shamefaced.

"Why?" Rick asked. "What was the point?"

When Brenda didn't answer, Nancy spoke

up. "It was for publicity. Brenda wanted to make a splash with her new column, so she invented an exciting, dramatic scenario. Right, Brenda?"

Brenda lifted her head and tossed back her dark hair. "Well, it *could* have happened," she said indignantly. "People need to know that things like that can happen. In a way, you could say I was just being a responsible journalist."

"Come off it, Brenda," Rick said angrily. He moved to the edge of the pool and sat down with his back to Brenda, his feet dangling in the water.

Brenda seemed to have lost some of her spirit as she turned to Rick. "I had to do it," she said, pleading to his back. "My father threatened to cancel my column because I wasn't getting any interesting mail. I figured if I got just one exciting letter, others would follow. So I decided to write one myself. I'm sorry," she added weakly. "I never meant for it to get out of hand like this."

That reminded Nancy of something she had wondered about. "Brenda, how did you come up with that particular letter?"

"I got the idea after the crash in the parking lot. Mrs. Keating kept talking about how her brakes weren't working, and I thought, suppose they were deliberately sabotaged?" She shrugged and seemed to be faintly pleased with herself. "The idea just took off from there."

"I thought that might be it," Nancy murmured, shaking her head. "I should've listened to my instincts."

"I couldn't believe it when Rick told me about his aunt, and I realized I had made up a story that was actually happening!" Brenda went on. Nancy noticed that she made it sound as if she'd done something really great.

A moment later, however, Brenda's expression deflated as she glanced at Rick, who had been sitting silently by the edge of the pool. Beams of late-afternoon sunlight shimmered on the surface of the water and outlined his slumped figure with a golden glow.

Nancy saw Brenda bite her lip uncertainly. Then the reporter rose from the chaise longue and went to sit beside Rick. She made little swirls in the water with her feet and stared down at them, as if unable to face Rick directly.

"Rick, I really am sorry," she said softly.

Nancy and Ned looked at each other in surprise. Brenda actually sounded humbled!

"I know I shouldn't have left you in the dark the way I did. I should have told you from the beginning that the letter was a fake." Brenda laid her hand on Rick's arm.

"The thing was," she went on, "when I first met you, I didn't want to tell you the truth because I was worried you'd tell people and then my column would be ruined. Then, when you told me about your aunt, I thought I really could help." Her eyes flashed defiantly as she snapped her head back at Nancy. "I *still* think I can help—if you want me to, that is." Brenda's voice faltered as she added, "I guess the real reason I didn't tell you is because I knew you'd be upset. I was afraid you'd think I was a terrible person."

"What does it matter to you what I think?" Rick asked her.

Brenda was obviously on the verge of tears. "It matters. I—I really think you're terrific, Rick. I know you probably don't feel the same about me after what I did, but I wanted to tell you that anyway."

Nancy never thought she'd see Brenda acting in a sincere and sensitive manner. She must be in love!

Rick turned to Brenda with a shy smile. "Hey, it's okay. I wish you'd told me sooner, but I guess there's no harm done."

From his deck chair Ned put in, "The question is, where do we go from here?"

Nancy leaned forward and propped her elbows on her knees, her attention once more on the case. She quickly told the others about her visit to Mrs. Keating. "She seemed pretty scared, but what I don't get is, if she's afraid her husband's going to kill her, why doesn't she go to the police?" Turning to Rick, she asked, "What do *you* think? You see them every day. How do they act toward each other? What's the atmosphere in the house?"

"Tense," Rick replied without hesitating. "Aunt Maggie's been on edge in general. But I don't know if it's because she thinks Uncle Bill is trying to kill her or if something totally different is bothering her. Uncle Bill seems pretty jumpy, too. I asked Aunt Maggie about it, but she just said he was under a lot of pressure at work."

"That doesn't mean much," Ned commented. He cleared his throat. "Phew! I'm thirsty. Sitting out here in the sun has dried me out."

"I have an idea," Brenda said, shaking the water from her feet and standing up. "Let's go get a soda and finish this discussion in a nice, air-conditioned restaurant. I want to take my car for a spin, anyway. It's just back from the shop, and I want to make sure it's running okay."

"Let's take my car," Nancy said to Ned as Rick and Brenda went into the bathhouse to change. "I should probably go straight home from the restaurant if I want to be on time for dinner." Flashing Ned a wide smile, she asked, "Want to come over? Hannah's making home-made strawberry ice cream for dessert."

"I'll be there," Ned said enthusiastically.

A few moments later Rick and Brenda reappeared, Brenda in a yellow minidress that showed off her tan, and Rick in shorts and a T-shirt.

"I have to get my car out of the garage," Brenda announced. Slipping her arm through Rick's, she suggested, "How about riding with me, Rick?"

"Those two are getting pretty cozy, aren't they?" Nancy remarked in a low voice as she and Ned followed Brenda and Rick around to the three-car garage at the top of the driveway.

"Mmm." Ned chuckled. "I hope he knows what he's getting into."

"Actually, I'm sort of glad for Brenda," Nancy said. "She really seems to like Rick. And he's a nice guy. It could be good for her to be around someone like him. She might learn something. You know, Brenda isn't dumb, even if she acts it most of the time. And she's very pretty—"

"She sure is," Ned put in.

"Ned!" Nancy exclaimed, but then she saw the teasing twinkle in his brown eyes. "You'd better watch out, Nickerson," she said, giving him a playful jab in the arm. "I almost took you seriously. Then you would have been in trouble!"

Just then Brenda's red sports car rolled out of the garage. "Nancy, follow me," Brenda called through the open window.

Nancy and Ned got in her Mustang, and Nancy pulled in behind Brenda.

"This driveway would be great for sledding

in the winter," Ned remarked as they drove down the hill. "It's steep, and it barely has any curves."

"How can you even think about winter when it's this hot out?" Nancy said, shaking her head in amazement. When he didn't answer, she glanced sideways and saw that Ned was peering through the windshield at Brenda's car, a slight frown creasing his brow.

"She's going too fast to make the turn at the bottom," he mumbled.

"Brenda drives the way she talks," Nancy replied. "Fast and—"

Nancy's voice broke off as Brenda's brake lights suddenly flashed on. With a screech of tires her red car fishtailed wildly across the driveway.

"Something's wrong!" Nancy cried, braking. "Brenda's car is out of control!"

Nancy watched helplessly as the red sports car barreled out of the drive and straight across the street. Then, with a terrible crunch, it slammed headlong into a huge tree!

Chapter

Ten

O<small>H, NO</small>!" Nancy cried. She jammed on the Mustang's emergency brake, threw off her seat belt, and jumped out of the car. Ned's footsteps echoed right behind her on the pavement as she raced toward Brenda's car.

The red sports car had thrown up a huge cloud of dust when it plowed into the dry earth around the tree. At first it was hard to see through the dense cloud.

"Brenda! Rick!" Nancy yelled, coughing from all the dust as she and Ned reached the car.

Ned yanked open the driver's side door and pulled at Brenda's safety belt. A moment later she fell out into his arms. "I couldn't turn the wheel!" Brenda cried. "I lost control!"

"Rick?" Nancy called, alarmed. She bent down and peered into the interior.

Rick was in the passenger seat, still wearing his seat belt. He stared at Nancy with a dazed expression. "I'm okay," he said. Then he managed a shaky grin. "It's a good thing I remembered to buckle up."

"Boy, am I glad you did," Nancy said fervently. She hurried around to his side and helped him out of the car. "Are you hurt at all?"

"I don't think so." Rick rubbed his neck gingerly. "My head snapped back when we hit the tree, but it doesn't feel too bad."

Rick's knees were wobbly, so Nancy supported him with an arm around his waist. They went around to the driver's side, where Brenda stood shivering, her arms crossed tightly across her chest and her dark eyes brimming with tears. "Three times in three days," she said.

It took Nancy a moment to make sense of what the reporter was saying. But then she realized it was true—the crash in the parking lot, the beam falling inside the mall, and now this. Could they *all* be accidents?

"What happened?" Nancy asked gently.

"I don't know," Brenda answered, turning to face Nancy. "I just couldn't move the steering wheel. It felt as if there were a heavy weight on it." The tears spilled over and ran down her cheeks. "And—and I was going too fast to stop—" She broke into a sob, and Rick put an arm around her shoulders.

"The whole thing happened like that," he said, snapping his fingers. "We didn't even have time to react."

Brenda dried her eyes on the back of her hand, then looked at Ned and Nancy. "I thought the wheel felt stiff when I took the car out of the garage," she explained. "I didn't pay any attention to it, though. Then all of a sudden we were flying down the hill, and I couldn't turn." Her lip quivered again. "I hit the brakes, but we still crashed."

Nancy didn't like the sound of that, but she kept quiet. No use scaring Brenda for no reason. "If you hadn't slammed on the brakes," she said reassuringly, "the accident would have been a lot more serious. Come on, let's get over to my car. You two need to sit and calm down."

Once Brenda and Rick were seated in Nancy's car, Nancy, keeping her voice light and casual, said, "Ned and I'll be right back. I just want to take a look under your hood, Brenda."

"Okay." Brenda was holding Rick's hand tightly. She still looked frightened, but Nancy thought she seemed to be recovering from her scare—and that she was definitely enjoying Rick's attention.

As they crossed the street again, Ned asked Nancy in a low voice, "What's going on? Do you think there's something wrong with Brenda's car?"

Nancy simply shrugged. She'd had a sudden, frightening idea, but it was such a long shot she didn't want to tell Ned about it until she checked it out.

The red car had hit the tree hard, but fortunately Brenda hadn't been going fast enough to do much damage. Ned managed to raise the hood without too much trouble, and they peered inside at the tangle of bolts, fans, and hoses.

"Uh-oh," Nancy said after a moment, frowning. Reaching down, she tapped on a white plastic container that was bolted to the car's chassis. "Look at that, Ned."

"Wow!" he exclaimed, grimacing. The container looked as if someone had attacked it with a buzz saw. The plastic was ripped to shreds. Thick yellowish fluid oozed sluggishly down the sides. "That's the steering fluid reserve," he said.

"You mean it used to be," Nancy amended. "No wonder Brenda couldn't turn the wheel," she said grimly. "The hydraulic system that controls her power steering is completely wrecked.

"Ned, is there any way this damage could have happened when Brenda hit the tree?" Nancy asked.

"No way," he told her. Ned gave a tight smile. "I'd say we're definitely looking at a case of sabotage."

Nancy took a deep breath. "That's what I

was afraid of. Listen, I don't want to say anything to Brenda until I know for sure," she added, biting her lip. "She's already practically hysterical about what just happened. First I want to check out the lock on her garage door and see if it's been tampered with. If not, I suppose there's still a chance that this happened by accident at the garage."

"If any garage is hiring mechanics who can shred a steering fluid unit that way by accident," Ned retorted as they walked back to the Mustang, "then I hope I never take my car there for repairs."

"What were you two doing over there?" Brenda asked as soon as Nancy and Ned walked up. "Why were you looking at my engine?"

"We just wanted to check something out," Nancy replied evasively. "Come on, let's go back up to your house."

"What were you checking out?" Brenda persisted as they all trudged back up the long hill. Her voice had regained its sharp edge. "You'd better tell me. It's my car, after all."

Rick took Brenda's hand. "I'm sure she'd let you know if there was anything to worry about."

Nancy was amazed by the way Brenda seemed to respond to Rick. A big smile spread across Brenda's face, and for the rest of the way up to the Carlton house, she was silent.

"Now what are you doing?" Brenda called

when Nancy and Ned headed for the garage. She hurried after them. "You guys are being awfully mysterious."

Nancy was already bending down to examine the lock on the garage door. It was just as she had guessed. The edges of the metal lock plate had several shiny new scratches. Someone had taken the plate off and picked the lock.

Nancy's mouth was set in a grim line as she turned to Brenda and Rick. "Okay. It's time I told you the whole story," she said.

"Whole story?" Rick repeated, faintly alarmed.

Nancy nodded, then made direct eye contact with Brenda. "That 'accident' you had just now was no accident," she said quietly.

"Your steering fluid container was slashed," Ned explained.

Brenda's mouth fell open.

"Is this a joke?" Rick asked incredulously, turning from Nancy to Ned.

"Sorry, but it's not," Nancy answered. She gestured at the lock on the garage door. "Someone picked this lock. I think we're looking at a case of sabotage."

"Oh, no. No way," Brenda burst out suddenly. "You're not going to pin this one on me!"

Nancy stared at her, mystified. "What are you—" she began.

But Brenda wasn't about to be interrupted. "I don't believe you!" she cried, angrily planting her hands on her hips. "You can't seriously think I'd stage something like this, just for the publicity. Wreck my own car? Put my life—and Rick's—in danger? I don't think so. Face it, Nancy. This accident was just as real as the one with the beam—" She broke off suddenly, the color draining from her face as the meaning of her own words sank in.

"Exactly," Nancy said. "I'm not trying to say you had anything to do with staging either accident, Brenda. But *someone* did."

"Oh," Brenda said in a tiny voice.

Rick gasped. "Are you saying someone really is trying to kill Brenda?" he demanded, horrified. "But why? What for?"

Raking a hand through her hair, Nancy explained, "The accident with the beam happened the day Brenda ran that phony letter in her column. I think seeing that letter upset someone."

She took a deep breath before saying, "It's only a guess, but if you ask me, all these accidents are further proof that there really *is* a murder scheme. Whoever's behind it thinks Brenda knows about it, so now he or she's trying to kill her, too!"

Chapter

Eleven

O<small>H, NO!</small>" Brenda wailed, burying her face in her hands. "I've got a murderer after me!"

Rick put his arms around Brenda and stroked her hair, but his attention was still focused on Nancy. "You're serious, aren't you?"

Nancy nodded.

"You think it's my uncle." It was a statement, not a question. "He really *is* trying to kill my aunt. And now he thinks Brenda knows, so he's trying to kill her, too." Rick's brilliant green eyes were troubled.

"There's no proof that it's your uncle," Nancy said cautiously. "At this point, for all we know it could be someone we've never even heard of. But from what you've told me about your aunt and uncle, and from what Ned and I found out about their insurance policies, it seems reasonable to start our investigation with them."

Brenda raised her head and glanced nervously over her shoulder. "I feel very exposed out here," she complained. "The murderer could be lurking right now, waiting for another chance to get me!"

Nancy grimaced at Brenda's overly dramatic flair, but she had to admit the reporter had a point.

"Why don't we go inside," Nancy suggested. "We can discuss what to do next over some cold drinks."

The four trooped inside the big white house, and Brenda directed the maid to bring a tray of sodas to the den.

Unlike the rest of the house, the den had a warm, lived-in feeling. The furniture was mismatched but cozy looking, and the big desk was cluttered with papers and books. A few framed college degrees and journalism awards hung on the walls, and Nancy guessed this was where Brenda's father, Frazier Carlton, worked.

Ned collapsed gratefully into a deep, well-worn armchair. "Whew, the air conditioning feels fantastic," he said, wiping his brow. Then, looking at Nancy, he asked, "So what's the plan?"

"We need evidence to prove our theory," Nancy began. She sat in another chair while

Brenda and Rick plopped down on a leather couch. "There are several things we should be doing. I think—if it's okay with everyone— that we should divide up the tasks and work in teams."

"Rick and I will work together," Brenda said immediately.

"Brenda, I'm sorry," said Nancy. "But you can't be on any of the teams."

"What?" Brenda cried. "Are you still trying to get back at me for that phony letter, Nancy?"

"No," Nancy said, trying not to lose her patience. "Someone has already arranged at least one, maybe two deadly 'accidents' for you, Brenda. We have to assume the person is going to try again. Your best protection is to stay put and not get yourself into even more danger."

"Nancy's right," Rick said to Brenda. "You are in danger. We can't risk losing you."

Brenda's eyes had been flashing angrily while Nancy spoke, but at Rick's words she calmed down, obviously touched by his concern.

The maid came in with their refreshments just then. After she left, Nancy went on. "Rick, you're our inside man at the Keatings' house," she said. "You have two jobs. One is to keep an eye on your aunt and make sure nothing happens to her. The other is to find out what you can about your uncle. Does he have a study?"

Rick nodded. "He does a lot of work at home."

"Check it out," Nancy told him. "There may be a paper trail—you know, records or documents that prove he's got serious money problems."

"Got it," Rick said eagerly.

Nancy leaned back in the chair and stretched her long legs out in front of her. "I think I'll call Bess and George in on this, too," she said. "They can go around to Mrs. Keating's hairdresser and places like that and scout out some gossip on her." She held up a hand to silence Rick, who was looking indignant. "You'd be surprised at how much people know about other people's private concerns," she said. "We may learn something useful."

Ned swallowed some soda and set his glass down. "What about you and me, Nan?" he asked.

"Don't worry," Nancy told him, smiling. "I have it all figured out." She turned to Rick. "Do you know where your aunt's car was towed after the accident with Brenda?"

He thought for a moment. "A place called Westlake Auto, I'm pretty sure."

"Is it still there?" Nancy asked.

Rick nodded. "It should be. They aren't scheduled to start work on it until tomorrow. Why?"

"Because that's where Brenda's car is going for repairs," Nancy told him.

"I don't use Westlake," Brenda protested.

"For now, you do," Nancy told her, grinning. "Have the car brought in under my name. That'll give Ned and me a chance to get in and look at Mrs. Keating's brakes."

"I don't see why *I* couldn't do that," Brenda muttered sulkily. "It wouldn't be dangerous."

"Too risky," Nancy said firmly. Turning to Ned, she said, "We'd better go. There's nothing more we can do tonight, and anyway, we're late for dinner."

As they were leaving, Nancy looked back at Brenda. The pretty brunette was standing on the porch with Rick, watching them go. Nancy didn't miss the determined, rebellious expression on Brenda's face.

Uh-oh. She's going to make trouble before this case is over, Nancy thought. I just know it.

Nancy cradled the receiver of her phone between her chin and shoulder and dialed George's number. Then she sat back on her bed, counting the rings until her friend answered.

"Hi," she said when George picked up after the third one.

"Hey, Nan. Great timing. Bess is over, and she's dying to talk to you!"

"What for?" Nancy asked.

"Uh, I think she wants to tell you herself,"

George warned, laughing. Then her voice became fainter as she said, "Okay, okay, I'm giving you the phone! Stop grabbing."

"What's going on?" Nancy asked.

"I'll tell you what's going on," came Bess's voice over the line. "I had a date with David Park last night! Did you get my message?"

"Oh!" Suddenly Nancy remembered Hannah's giving her the message from Bess the day before. She'd been so preoccupied with the case that she had totally forgotten to return Bess's call the night before. "Oh, Bess, I'm sorry," she said sincerely. "I got it. I just had a lot on my mind."

"Mmmm. I'm not surprised," Bess replied. "I could see it coming the other night at the concert. You have a new case, don't you?"

"Guilty," Nancy admitted with a laugh.

"So—what is this case?" Bess asked.

Nancy could hear George's voice faintly in the background. "A new case? Tell her to come over and fill us in, pronto. She's not about to do anything without our help!"

A warm feeling spread through Nancy. She could always count on Bess and George. They were the greatest!

"I'll tell you about it in a second," she said to Bess. "But first, I want to hear all the details of your date!"

"So what do we do, Nan?" Ned whispered.

"I'm not sure," Nancy admitted. She

stepped around a heap of oily engine parts, carefully holding the hem of her white dress away from them. "I guess we'll have to improvise."

It was ten-thirty in the morning, and Nancy and Ned were standing by Brenda's car, amid a hum of activity, at Westlake Auto. Ned had taken the morning off so that he could go with Nancy to check out the brakes on Mrs. Keating's car.

Nancy frowned, considering. "We can't just tell the mechanic we suspect the brakes were sabotaged," she said quietly. "He'll think we're crazy!"

She straightened away from Ned as a harassed-looking man in stained white coveralls walked toward them, wiping his hands on a rag. The name Ernie was embroidered on a patch on his chest.

"Can I help you folks?" the man asked.

"Yes. Uh, I'm Nancy Drew," she began hesitantly. "I—"

The mechanic interrupted her, scowling. "Oh, you're the one who owns this car. Look, I didn't appreciate your attitude on the phone yesterday."

What was he talking about? Nancy wondered. Then she realized Brenda must have said something rude to the guy. "But I—" she began again.

Ernie cut her off. "I'm sorry, but there's no way I'll be able to get to your car before tomorrow." He waved a hand at the crowded shop. "You can see how backed up we are. We're so busy I can't even keep track of what my men are doing."

The place did seem a little frantic. Men in white Westlake Auto coveralls hurried back and forth among dozens of cars in the huge space. As she looked around, Nancy had an idea.

She was wearing white, too. If Ned could keep Ernie occupied, she could find Mrs. Keating's car and look at the brakes. In the bustle the odds were that no one would notice her.

"Oh, but you *have* to fix the car today," she whined. "We need it." She grasped Ned's arm possessively. "Today is our one-year anniversary, and this is the car that we rode in on our very first date. We have such a big day planned, and if I don't get to ride in this car *today,* I'll just have a *fit!*" She squeezed Ned's arm. "Honey, can't you talk to him?"

Ned glanced down at her in surprise, and Nancy gave him a discreet kick on the ankle.

"Er—that's right," Ned said quickly. He leaned toward Ernie, lowering his voice. "Let me tell you, you don't want to be around this girl when she's having a fit. It's not a pretty sight." Looking back at Nancy, he shot her a quick wink.

Oooh! I'll get him for that later, she thought.

Ernie's expression was doubtful. "All the same," he said, "I can't get to it right away."

"Oh, *please!*" Nancy made her lower lip tremble. "If our plans are ruined I'll—I'll cry."

Ned put an arm around Ernie's shoulder. "Can we talk about this for a minute, man to man?" Still talking, he led Ernie toward the office.

Nancy watched them go, stifling a laugh. Not bad! Now I'd better get to it before they come back.

It took only a few seconds for her to recognize Mrs. Keating's silver sedan. It was parked near the back of the garage. As she wandered over, Nancy saw a pair of legs in white coveralls poking out from under the car's body. Someone was apparently working on it already.

That's probably good, Nancy realized. If she played this right, she could even get an expert's opinion on Mrs. Keating's brake trouble.

Bending down, Nancy said, "Excuse me."

There was a clattering sound as the mechanic slid out from under the car on a small, wheeled board. He stood up, dusting off his hands. Then he raised his eyes straight at Nancy. Her heart leapt into her throat.

"You!" she cried.

She was facing the man with the mismatched eyes!

Chapter

Twelve

THE MAN gave Nancy a quizzical smile and asked, "Have we met?" But she was sure she saw a glint of recognition in his eyes.

Her thoughts were in a whirl, and her gaze kept flicking back and forth between the man's blue and brown eyes. In all the excitement of Brenda's accident, she'd completely forgotten him. Yet he'd been at the mall the day of Brenda's first car accident and near the Keatings' house the night of the concert. What was he doing working on Mrs. Keating's car now?

"No, you don't know me," Nancy responded after a moment. "But I've seen you before." She decided not to mention anything about seeing Rick chase him the night of the Ice Planet concert.

"You seemed very interested in an accident involving this car," she went on carefully.

"Ah, of course. You were the good Samaritan," the man said easily. "How could I forget a face as pretty as yours?" He unzipped his coveralls and stepped out of them. Underneath, Nancy noted, he had on an expensive-looking suit.

"Oh, I don't actually work here," he explained when he saw her look of surprise. "I just slipped in and—er—borrowed this extra coverall when the office was empty."

Nancy folded her arms, unsure of what to make of the guy. He was smooth—almost too smooth—and she didn't really trust him. "Why?" she asked bluntly.

The man shrugged. "It was more convenient than trying to explain to the mechanics that I wanted to examine one of their cars to see if its brakes had been doctored."

"What?" Nancy couldn't contain her surprise.

"Well, surely you suspect the same thing," the man said in a reasonable voice. "After all, you were the one who told Maggie to get her brakes checked in the first place."

From the familiar way he used Mrs. Keating's name, Nancy guessed he knew her. "Just who are you?" she demanded. "And what are you up to?"

"Oh, excuse my rudeness," the man said

with a charming laugh. He held out his hand. "I'm Maggie Keating's brother-in-law. Name's Chris Trout."

Brother-in-law? Suddenly Nancy recalled her father telling her that Mrs. Keating was the widow of a lawyer named Wilford Trout. This guy must be Wilford's younger brother. But what was he doing in the garage?

Reaching out, she took Trout's hand and shook it. "I'm Nancy Drew," she told him.

"Delighted," Trout said in that same supersmooth tone. Reaching into the pocket of the coveralls, he drew out a flat, oddly shaped piece of silvery metal. "Well, Nancy, you can be my witness. This is the proof that Maggie's brakes were sabotaged. I just found it."

Nancy's mind was racing. What was Trout up to? Could he somehow be involved in the plot to kill Mrs. Keating? He had been at the mall when she ran into Brenda. Could that be a coincidence? Nancy had to find out more!

"I didn't see you find that thing," she pointed out, hoping to goad more information from him. "Anyway, I don't even know what it is. You say it's proof of sabotage, but how do I know you're telling the truth?"

"Very good!" Trout said approvingly. He held the piece of metal up so Nancy could examine it. "This is a brake shoe. Notice the wear here and here." He pointed to two uneven spots on the surface of the metal piece and went on to explain, "Now, wear is usual in everyday driving but not quite like this. If you look closely, you can see file marks."

Nancy caught her breath. He was right!

"It's very subtle, though." Raising his eyebrows, Trout added, "I doubt a regular auto mechanic would even catch it. It's just that I have some expertise on the subject of brakes."

"How so?" Nancy asked cautiously.

"I drive Formula One race cars," Trout told her. He made a sigh that seemed a little exaggerated. "Unfortunately, racing is a very expensive hobby, what with the cost of the cars themselves, maintenance, entry fees, and so forth. I've been forced into temporary retirement, due to lack of funds."

His mismatched eyes held a strange gleam as he added, "But my luck may be changing. I think you can look for me on the racetrack again in the near future."

More questions whirled in Nancy's head. Was he making some weird reference to the plan to kill Mrs. Keating? But then, why would he tell her about the sabotaged brakes if he was in on the plot? Unless he just wanted her to *think* he was trying to protect Mrs. Keating to throw Nancy off the track—

Nancy shook herself. It was all guesswork until she came up with proof. Clearing her throat, she said, "About the brake shoe—"

"Oh, yes. The brake shoe." Trout looked

down at the object in his hand, then gave Nancy a sudden, wolfish grin. "Don't worry. I'll make sure the proper people see it."

Before Nancy could even open her mouth to ask what he meant, Trout strode jauntily away.

"Nancy, I think we're going to have to give up for today," Ned's voice came from behind her.

Startled, Nancy turned around. Ned stood there with the mechanic.

"What?" Nancy asked, her mind still on the strange conversation with Trout.

"I said, I think we're going to have to give up on getting the car fixed today," Ned replied.

"Well, we'll live," Nancy said distractedly.

"Gee, you're sure you're not too disappointed?" Ned asked, frowning at her.

Suddenly Nancy remembered they were supposed to be putting on an act for Ernie. "Oh, of course I am," she said, pouting. "I'm *very* disappointed. Ned, let's go. I think I'm going to cry."

Doing her best to look upset, Nancy led the way out of the garage. As soon as they were around the corner and out of sight, though, she grabbed Ned's hand. "Listen to this!" Quickly she filled him in on her encounter with Chris Trout.

Ned whistled when she was done. "This Trout guy sounds like bad news," he commented.

"I agree," Nancy said. "He acted like he

wanted to help, but—I don't know, I got the feeling he was hiding something. If he really wanted to help Mrs. Keating, why would he run off like that with the brake shoe? Maybe he's actually in on some plan with Mr. Keating." Her blue eyes had a determined gleam in them as she added, "One thing's for sure."

"What's that?" Ned inquired.

"I've got some homework to do on both Bill Keating and Chris Trout."

"Wow, Nancy," Bess said wistfully. "This guy Chris Trout sounds kind of romantic."

"I don't know," said George. She poured herself a refill of soda and went back to her seat at the Drews' kitchen table. "Sometimes the most charming guys are the ones who make the most trouble."

Nancy nodded her agreement. "The question is, what kind of trouble?"

The girls had just eaten dinner, and now they were comparing notes on what they had learned that day.

"He's definitely a slippery kind of guy," Nancy went on. "The only solid information he gave me was that he drives Formula Ones—you know, race cars. So I called some racing people, and they actually thought I was trying to track Trout down for money. The guy said something like, 'Look, lady, you'll have to wait in line behind me and half of Chicago.'"

"Maybe he's not so romantic after all," Bess commented, taking a sip of soda.

"But it sounds like he's definitely broke," said George.

"Right," Nancy said with a nod. "I called my dad about it, and he told me both Wilford and Chris Trout inherited a lot of money from their parents. But both of them let it slip away within just a few years. Wilford still made good money as a lawyer, though, and my dad says Wilford was always giving money to Chris. I wonder if Chris hoped Wilford's widow would continue with the handouts," she added, thinking out loud.

"Maybe he's trying to kill Mrs. Keating and get it blamed on Mr. Keating so that he can inherit whatever she has," Bess suggested. "Ugh," she added, shuddering.

"That doesn't make sense unless Mrs. Keating put a special provision for Chris in her will," Nancy pointed out. "He's not Mrs. Keating's next of kin. He's not even really related to her."

"Besides," said George, "from what I heard today, I don't think Mrs. Keating has much money to leave to anyone."

Nancy nodded. "That's what Rick said, too. What exactly did you find out?"

"Well, I talked to Mrs. Keating's hairdresser, Maurice," began George, reaching for the last of Hannah's chocolate chip cookies. "He has this chic salon, but he was pretty chatty. I went in to talk to him about a new look." She grinned and patted her dark curls.

"You didn't!" Bess cried admiringly. "Oh, this sounds fun. I wish I'd rescheduled my dentist's appointment so I could have gone with you."

George crunched into the cookie, then went on with her story. "After a while I got the conversation around to Mrs. Keating," she said. "Maurice is upset with her because she bounced three checks in a row. He says that right before Mrs. Keating married Mr. Keating, she was talking a lot about how much money she was going to have after the wedding. Maurice thinks *she* married him for *his* money."

"Now, that's interesting," Nancy said. "It's beginning to look as if both Mr. and Mrs. Keating went into their marriage thinking the other one would make them wealthy again."

"And they were both disappointed," Bess added excitedly. "Hey, maybe they're trying to kill each other!"

Nancy smiled at Bess. "Maybe," she allowed. "But so far we have no evidence that anyone is trying to kill *Mr.* Keating."

The three girls turned as Ned appeared in the kitchen doorway. "Hannah let me in," he explained. "What's up?"

Nancy was about to start filling him in when the telephone rang. She reached for the kitchen extension. "Hello?"

It was Brenda. She was beside herself with excitement. "Guess what?" she cried. "I just got an anonymous phone tip!"

"What?" Nancy asked. "Calm down, Brenda. What are you talking about?"

"It happened just five minutes ago," Brenda said. "The phone rang, and when I picked it up, this muffled voice told me I could get information that would help the woman who wrote the letter in my column. All I have to do is show up at Bluff Bridge at nine o'clock tonight."

"Brenda," Nancy said sternly, feeling a prickle of unease, "the letter was a fake, remember? This could be a trap."

"I know that!" Brenda said scornfully. "I'm not an idiot, Nancy. I'm just calling to tell you I'm going to set a trap for *him.*"

"You can't go!" Nancy yelled into the receiver. Was Brenda actually dumb enough to try to outsmart a potential murderer? Then Nancy remembered something. "Your car's still in the shop," she pointed out, heaving a sigh of relief. "You don't have any way to get there."

There was a sulky silence. "Well, how are we going to catch this guy?" Brenda asked at last.

Nancy glanced at her watch. It was already eight thirty-five! "I'll go in your place," she said, thinking fast. "I'll take Ned. And can you call Rick? Tell him to be on the far side of the bridge at ten of nine—and to watch for anyone approaching from that side."

After slamming down the phone, Nancy grabbed Ned and herded him toward the door. "I'll explain later, you guys," she called back to Bess and George.

In the car she told Ned about her conversation with Brenda. "We're going to set a trap for the 'trapper,'" she finished.

"Let's just try to stay alive until we get there," Ned said, sounding worried. "You're going awfully fast, Nancy."

"We have to beat him there," Nancy insisted, maintaining her speed.

At eight fifty-two Nancy parked in the shadow of some trees by the bridge. The steel arc soared high over the Muskoka River, with tall cliffs on either side. A few yellow street lamps gave it little light.

"You stay out of sight and guard this end of the bridge," she told Ned. "Rick should be on the other side. I'll go meet our mystery man."

"Nan, be careful," Ned said. He kissed her.

"I will," she promised.

Taking a deep breath, she walked toward the bridge. It appeared to be deserted, but there were plenty of dark, shadowy areas at both ends. Gnarled old trees hung out over the bridge, curtaining it off in a way that Nancy found sinister. She didn't like to think it, but a dangerous man could be hiding within just a few feet of her.

Her senses extra-alert, Nancy walked under the curtain of trees and stepped onto the bridge. She paused to look around, struck by the odd feeling that someone was watching her. It's just Ned and Rick, she told herself sternly.

Nancy had taken a few more steps out onto the bridge when suddenly something thudded down behind her. Nancy jumped to one side— but not fast enough.

Hands slammed into her back and shoved her violently. Before she could do more than scream, Nancy found herself lurching forward, then falling—right over the guardrail of the bridge!

Chapter

Thirteen

NANCY FELT the blood rush to her head as she slid headfirst over the side of the bridge, her legs scraping against the sharp edge of the rail.

"Help!"

She twisted her body in midair, and her hands shot out to make one desperate grab at a steel post. In a flash the metal was slipping through her palms, and Nancy clenched her teeth in despair.

Then, her scrabbling fingers locked around an edge of the post, and with a wrenching jerk her body stopped its fall. Pain shot through her arms, and she saw white stars behind her closed eyelids. But she wasn't falling any longer!

Panting, Nancy hung onto the post. After a

moment she worked up the courage to open her eyes. She was dangling below the level of the roadbed, amid a crisscrossing mesh of support beams and girders. Wind moaned through the steel web and whipped her hair into her eyes.

She risked a cautious peep downward—and immediately wished she hadn't. A hundred feet below, the Muskoka sent back a faint reflection of the bridge's lights. One small slip, and she'd be history!

The wind gusted, pulling at Nancy's entire body. Her heart jumped as she felt her fingers slip a fraction of an inch. She wouldn't be able to hang on much longer. Think clearly, Drew, she ordered herself.

Above her there was a confused babble of voices. Nancy tried to cry for help, but all that came out was a faint croak. Swallowing to moisten her dry throat, she tried again. "Help me!"

"Nancy?" Rick Waterston's blond head poked out over the rail. "Oh, no!" he cried as he spotted her. In an instant he had swung his long legs over the rail and was climbing down the girders. "Hang on! I'm coming!" he shouted.

Nancy's hand slipped again, until she now clung by just the tips of her fingers. "Hurry!" she called back frantically. "I'm about to fall!"

The wind gusted again, and Nancy's heart lurched as the metal bar slipped away from her fingers. Just in time Rick's strong hand closed around her left wrist.

"I'm going to pull you up," Rick told her. "Trust me—I've done a lot of climbing."

Nancy's breath came in heaving gulps. Talk about close calls! But she still wasn't out of trouble. Looking up she could see the strain in Rick's face as he hauled her up. At last she was high enough that her feet found a ledge to support her weight. Slowly, with Rick guiding her every inch of the way, she climbed up the web of metal and over the lip of the bridge. Finally she lay collapsed on the road, gasping.

"Thanks," she said to Rick when she could speak again. "You saved my life."

"Don't thank me. I blew it," he said gruffly. "And our man clobbered Ned and got away before I could grab him."

"Is Ned hurt?" Nancy asked anxiously.

"I don't know. Brenda's checking," Rick said.

"Brenda?" Nancy repeated, suddenly wary. "What's she doing here?"

At that moment Brenda herself appeared from the shadows, supporting a limping, scowling Ned.

Jumping to her feet, Nancy ran to him and threw her arms around him. "Ned, are you okay?"

"I'm all right." Ned held her close. He spoke lightly, but Nancy heard a tremor in his voice. "I thought you were a goner, though, Nan."

"I'm fine," she assured him. "Now, tell me what happened."

Ned's face immediately darkened again. "Ask Brenda. She's the only one who saw anything, after that stupid camera flash of hers blinded me."

"Brenda!" Nancy exclaimed.

Beside Ned, Brenda flipped her dark hair back defiantly. "I was only trying to help," she muttered. "I thought it might be a good idea to come and get a picture, in case you guys let the crook get away."

"He wouldn't have gotten away if I had been able to see him!" Ned retorted furiously. "But I couldn't see a thing. The guy swung out of the trees and attacked you," he told Nancy. "I was running for him when Brenda popped up behind him and clicked her camera. The flash went off in my eyes, and the guy bolted. On the way he took time to flatten me." Ned rubbed his jaw and winced.

"Brenda, how did you get here?" Nancy asked, facing her.

Brenda's eyes flicked toward Rick, who stepped up beside Nancy.

"I brought her," Rick confessed in response to Nancy's questioning glance. "She really wanted to come, and I didn't think it would do any harm as long as she stayed in the car." He gave Brenda an angry look. "You promised you would," he reminded her.

Brenda hung her head and said nothing.

"Well," Nancy said with a sigh, "it's done. At least none of us got seriously hurt." Turning to Brenda, she added, "Get your film developed right away," she said. "Maybe there'll be a clear shot of our mystery man."

"Why do you keep calling him the mystery man?" Rick wanted to know. "There's no question that it's Uncle Bill, is there?"

"Yes, there is," Nancy told him. "First, we still have no hard evidence that this case involves the Keatings at all. Second," she went on, thinking out loud as she spoke, "even if it does involve them, there's still a lot of unexplained stuff going on. I'm pretty sure Chris Trout fits into this, but I'm not sure how."

She turned to Rick, remembering something else. "You knew it was him outside your aunt's house the other night," she said. "Why didn't you want to admit it?"

Rick's face took on an apologetic expression. "I didn't even know Uncle Wilford's brother was around until you described him. I couldn't figure out what he was doing there, but the whole thing really got me scared. Aunt Maggie's been so afraid to talk about what's going on that I guess I just clammed up, too. I was afraid something terrible might happen if I said anything—I'm not sure why."

He shook his head slowly, as if confused by his own actions. "And then I was so freaked out by Brenda's accident and what you told me about my aunt's insurance, I forgot all about Uncle Chris."

"Well, there's a chance he could have set up this meeting," Nancy said, trying to piece things together in her mind. She thought of the brake shoe and Trout's words about getting it to "the right people." Could he have meant Brenda? But why would he want to give it to her?

"Speaking of hard evidence," Rick said, breaking into Nancy's train of thought, "all I found when I searched Uncle Bill's study today is evidence that he's weird."

"What do you mean?" Ned asked him.

Rick shrugged. "He has this folder full of clippings. Mostly it was stuff about the military, but there were lots of articles about tornadoes."

"Tornadoes?" Nancy was puzzled.

"Well, not tornadoes, exactly," Rick corrected himself. "Actually, they were all about microbursts. You know, those minitornadoes that all the meteorologists are warning about these days. The ones that appear out of nowhere, zap your house, and disappear before you even see what hit you." He grinned sourly. "Maybe Uncle Bill is trying to come up with some way to develop them into the army's newest secret weapon."

"Maybe." Nancy let out a heavy sigh. Her

head was beginning to pound, and she couldn't think straight anymore. "Let's all go home," she told the others. "We can start again tomorrow, after we've seen Brenda's photographs."

The sound of the telephone awakened Nancy from a deep sleep the following morning. Through bleary eyes, she checked the clock on her bedside table. Ten o'clock. Then she reached for the phone and mumbled, "'Lo?"

It was Rick. "I'm at *Today's Times* with Brenda," he said. "We just developed the film from last night."

Nancy sat up in bed, shaking herself awake. "Anything?" she asked.

"Nope. It's useless," came Rick's unhappy voice. "She got one shot. It shows a blur which we think is the attacker's shoulder—but it could be something else. And there's a great shot of Ned looking surprised."

It wasn't exactly good news, but Rick sounded so down Nancy decided to try to cheer him up. "Look, why don't you two take a break. I'll figure out our next move."

After she hung up, Nancy got up and showered. She was a bit stiff from her adventure the night before, and the air seemed thick and close, even in the air-conditioned house. Glancing out the window, Nancy wasn't surprised to see that the sky had a yellowish cast to it.

Tornado watch today, I'll bet. Still wearing her towel, she went over to the clock-radio by her bed and switched it on.

"The watch is in effect for the Chicago area," the newscaster was saying. "And for you folks in the River Heights area, look out. Twisters have been sighted heading your way, and we have reports of at least two microbursts touching down. Fortunately, no casualties have been reported. For live coverage, we go now to . . ."

As she listened to the tornado warning, several things suddenly clicked into place. The tornadoes—the folder full of clippings about microbursts—

Nancy reached down and snapped off the radio, cutting off the newscaster's voice. Her mind was racing. She could hardly believe what she was thinking—it was too farfetched.

"Oh, no!" she groaned out loud. "Could he really do it?" She didn't know how, but she suspected Mr. Keating was somehow going to use the tornado warnings to fake some kind of fatal "accident" for his wife.

After throwing on a pair of jeans and a polo shirt, she raced downstairs and headed for the door.

"Nancy?" Hannah Gruen's voice came from the kitchen. "Don't you want any breakfast?"

"No time!" Nancy called over her shoulder. "I've got to stop a murder from happening!"

In her car Nancy floored the gas pedal. She smiled grimly. If Ned griped about my driving last night, it's good he's not with me now!

Five minutes later she pulled up the driveway to the Keatings' big Victorian house. There was only one car in the garage, a white station wagon. Seeing it made Nancy pause. Suddenly she realized she had no idea what she was going to do next.

Improvise, she told herself fiercely. A woman's life is at stake!

Nancy hurried up and rang the bell, and a moment later Mrs. Keating opened the door. She looked even more shaken up than when Nancy had spoken with her last, but at least she was alive!

"Hi," Nancy said, vastly relieved. "May I come in?" Without waiting for a reply, she bustled inside, herding Mrs. Keating in front of her.

"You may not remember me," she went on, speaking softly and quickly. "I'm Nancy Drew. I was there when you had the accident at the mall."

"Yes, of course," Mrs. Keating said. She was wringing her hands, and her large brown eyes had a look of tense bewilderment in them.

"We don't have much time," Nancy hurried on. "I know this will sound strange, but I think you'll have some idea of what I'm talking about."

"I'm afraid I don't have any idea yet."

"Look, I'm a detective. I know about your husband trying to kill you," Nancy said bluntly.

Mrs. Keating's brown eyes looked as if they might pop out of her head. "You—you know?" she whispered in a shaky voice.

"Yes. And I'm sorry to have to say this, but I think he's about to try again. You should leave the house right away. You're in danger here."

Mrs. Keating was still staring, not moving. Suddenly Nancy realized that the woman wasn't looking *at* her, but rather *behind* her. A sixth sense shouted at Nancy to turn around.

It was too late. As she started to turn, a thick cloth pad was clapped over her mouth and nose. She gasped as a bitter, acrid stench assaulted her nostrils.

Then, abruptly, there was blackness.

Chapter

Fourteen

NANCY SWAM SLOWLY UP through a sea of dark mist. "Oooh," she groaned as her eyes fluttered open. The inside of her head felt as if someone were pounding at it with a sledgehammer.

"What . . . ?" Gradually the objects around her came into focus, and Nancy realized she was in a leather recliner in a darkened room.

Where am I? she wondered, frowning.

Heavy velvet curtains shrouded the room's two big windows. To Nancy's left was a massive maple rolltop desk stacked with color-coded folders. Bookshelves flanked one wall, with a lumpy-looking velvet sofa in a shadowed recess between them. The adjoining wall was covered with framed photographs.

Feeling too weak to get out of the chair, Nancy squinted to bring the photos into focus.

Most of them were black-and-white group shots of men in uniform.

Soldiers . . . Bill Keating. Suddenly what just happened came flooding back.

She had come to warn Mrs. Keating. In her mind Nancy pictured the look of panic on Mrs. Keating's face—just before those hands came from behind and held the drug-soaked cloth over Nancy's mouth and nose to knock her out. She shuddered at the memory.

"I must be in the Keatings' house," she said aloud. In fact, she guessed she was in Mr. Keating's study. Keating must have come in and caught her, she realized. But what had become of Mrs. Keating?

A slight movement from the lumpy sofa made Nancy's eyes snap over to it. She hadn't noticed before because the couch was set back in the shadows, but now she made out a human form lying there!

Forcing herself up and out of the recliner, Nancy made her way painfully across to the sofa. "Mrs. Keating?"

Nancy's eyes widened as she saw not Mrs. Keating, but Chris Trout lying on the sofa. His eyes were closed, and even in the dim light she could see that he was deathly pale. A bruised swelling marked his forehead just above the left eye.

He's out cold, Nancy realized. But why? What's he doing here?

Suddenly a wave of dizziness hit her. She

had to grab on to the bookshelf to keep herself from falling over. Clenching her teeth, she held on and waited for the spell of nausea to pass.

This is bad, Drew. If you don't pull yourself together, you'll never get out of here!

As she gazed around the room, the dim sound of a car engine starting floated in through the window. Nancy went over as fast as her wobbly legs would carry her. Pulling aside the heavy red curtain, she gazed out, shielding her eyes from the abrupt rush of sunlight.

She saw that she was in a room on the second floor that looked out over the porch roof. The white station wagon that she had seen in the garage when she arrived was now in the driveway. As she watched, the driver's side door opened, and Bill Keating got out.

"Come on," he called, beckoning to someone who was apparently standing on the porch below Nancy. "We don't have time to argue about it now! Just get rid of the car. We can't leave any evidence that the girl was here. Then get out of sight!"

His words barely registered. Nancy tried to cut through the pounding fog in her head and think clearly. Whom was he talking to? She didn't have to wait long to find out. A second later someone hurried down the porch steps and ran to Nancy's car.

Mrs. Keating!

Nancy's stomach did a flip-flop. "Uh-oh,"

she muttered. "I think I've been missing one big piece of the puzzle."

She put a hand to her aching head. "Think, Drew!" she told herself, scowling fiercely. It wasn't easy. Whatever Keating had used to knock her out must have been pretty strong. But even in her weakened state, some very disturbing ideas were beginning to surface.

I came here thinking that Bill Keating was trying to kill Maggie Keating to collect her insurance money, she thought. And I got that idea from reading the letter in Brenda's column. But I know that Brenda made that letter up—it wasn't real. She didn't know anything about Mr. and Mrs. Keating when she wrote it.

So isn't it reasonable to assume that the letter wasn't right? Isn't it possible that Brenda got part of the plan right—but was wrong about other parts?

What if Mrs. Keating isn't Mr. Keating's victim after all? Nancy reasoned. What if she's his accomplice?

"Of course. Why not?" Nancy murmured. It made sense, in a sick way. Both Mr. and Mrs. Keating had married thinking that the other partner was rich, and Nancy's investigation had shown that both were disappointed. But instead of trying to kill each other, they had teamed up to remedy the situation!

It all clicked. "That's why Mrs. Keating didn't want the police to come when she had the accident with Brenda," Nancy said aloud. "That's why she wouldn't confide in Rick after she saw Brenda's letter in the paper. She wasn't afraid her husband was trying to kill her—she was afraid Brenda had found out about the plot to *fake* her death and collect that million dollars in insurance! She was afraid of being caught!"

That also explained the way Mrs. Keating had been staring behind Nancy just before Mr. Keating knocked her out. Nancy shook her head in amazement. She sure had misread the situation. Now that Nancy thought about it, she realized that the odd look on Mrs. Keating's face hadn't been panic—it had been expectation.

She was just waiting for her husband to sneak up on me, Nancy thought angrily. And I thought she was in trouble!

The roar of the Mustang's engine made Nancy look down at the driveway again. Mrs. Keating had started the car. As Nancy watched, she drove away.

Hey, that's my car! Nancy wanted to shout. But she didn't think it would do much good. Besides, she had more immediate problems. Obviously, the Keatings planned on getting rid of her. She had to get both herself and the unconscious Chris Trout out of there before Mr. Keating came back to finish them off!

Still feeling unsteady, Nancy went over to

the study door and tugged on the knob. It didn't turn. The door was locked, of course. She'd expected as much.

She bent down and examined the latch. Not pickable. She couldn't see the locking mechanism, but from the look of it it was the sort where a section of the doorknob turned, too. A one-way lock. Strange—usually those were set up so that a person could lock and unlock the door from *inside* the room.

I'll bet Mr. Keating just took this one off the door and switched it around, Nancy guessed. It wouldn't be hard, and it would keep us in here very efficiently.

Going over to one of the windows, she struggled to raise the sash, but it didn't budge. Then she noticed that two stout nails had been driven into the wooden sill from the outside. They were holding the window shut.

She gazed out through the glass. If she broke the window, maybe she could shout loud enough to get someone's attention. . . .

That hope faded as she remembered the thick belt of trees that surrounded the Keatings' property. The place was isolated. From where Nancy stood, she couldn't even see any other houses. No one would hear her cries.

Just then another wave of sick dizziness swept over Nancy. She gripped the doorknob, but the whirling feeling grew stronger. Gasping, she slid down the wall to the thickly carpeted floor and put her head between her knees.

She shook her head, trying to clear it, but if anything, she felt worse than she had five minutes earlier.

Suddenly she caught a whiff of that same bitter scent that she had smelled right before she lost consciousness. It was strangely familiar, but she couldn't place it. Nancy racked her fogged brain. I know that smell, but from where?

Just then a scene flashed into her head of her high-school chemistry lab. The teacher was holding up a beaker of some liquid and lecturing about it. "Quite dangerous . . . highly explosive . . ." And that same acrid taint hung faintly in the air. . . .

"Ether!" Nancy cried, snapping her fingers.

So that was what Keating had used to knock her out. He must have left some of it in the house, and the fumes were seeping into the air as it evaporated.

Nancy stood up and sniffed. The smell was strongest around the door and near the ceiling, so the ether was probably in the attic.

That was bad, she realized with a sinking heart. Besides the fact that the fumes were making her progressively weaker, if there were any sparks or open flames going anywhere in the house they might set off an explosion. . . .

Suddenly the war story she had heard Keating tell the other day in the bank rang in her ears with a dreadful significance. He had built ether bombs during the war. All it took was a bottle of ether and a lit candle. She could hear his voice, saying, "A few hours later the ether fumes reached the candle flame, and—boom!"

Nancy had a sudden, sinking feeling in the pit of her stomach. "So that's how he's going to do it," she whispered.

The entire attic is a bomb, and when it goes up, Trout and I go with it! The authorities will find a demolished house—and two very demolished bodies.

It was a horribly clever plan. Not only were the Keatings getting rid of Nancy, but they were also providing themselves with a stand-in for Mrs. Keating's body. Because all that would be left of Nancy were some unidentifiable remains!

Chapter

Fifteen

THAT'S WHY Mr. Keating had all those clippings about microbursts," Nancy said, thinking out loud.

She knew she was talking to herself. Over on the sofa Chris Trout still hadn't stirred. Somehow, though, hearing her own voice made her feel a little less alone.

"It was research," she said. "He's going to pretend that a minitornado touched down and demolished the house. It's perfect. No one can predict those things, and they touch down so fast that it's easy to miss them. Besides, there are no neighbors close enough to be witnesses.

"And that's why the ether bomb is up in the attic," she continued. "The house has to be wrecked from the top down, so that the microburst story will be convincing." She glanced over at Chris Trout. "And poor Mrs.

Keating and her brother-in-law just happened
to be in the study upstairs when it happened,"
she added grimly.

It was a horrible thought. Nancy shuddered.
"What am I going to do?" she asked.

She did have one thing going for her, she
realized. She was sure Keating hadn't expected
her to regain consciousness before the blast
came. That was why he hadn't tied her up.
He'd secured the doors and windows to mini-
mize the risk, but he couldn't chance tying
Nancy's arms and legs. If rope fragments were
found in the wreckage, that might raise awk-
ward questions.

She glanced over at Trout again. Still out.
She couldn't count on his help—he might not
wake up as long as they remained inside. The
ether fumes were keeping him under.

How much time do I have? Nancy wondered
desperately. She thought about Keating's story
again. He'd said the ether bomb took a few
hours to detonate. But the tunnel Keating had
blown up must have been huge, big enough to
hold an entire convoy of trucks. The Keatings'
house was much smaller. Even if the candle
flame was downstairs on the first floor, the
ether fumes would reach it much more
quickly.

Nancy felt a bone-chilling shiver. Groaning,
she sat down on the leather recliner and
dropped her head in her hands.

But then anger swept over her. "Get up,

Drew!" she told herself. She'd been in tight spots before. And she'd always found a way out. Nancy shook her head to clear it of useless doubts. She had no choice. She *had* to get them both out.

She stood up, ignoring the spots that were beginning to dance in front of her eyes. Grabbing Bill Keating's maple desk chair, she dragged it over to the nearer of the two windows.

All she had to do was pick it up and swing it through the glass. Come on, you can do it! she told herself.

But it looked so impossibly heavy, another part of her moaned.

"Do it!" she said out loud in a harsh voice.

With a tremendous effort Nancy picked up the wooden chair and heaved it forward, smashing it into the glass pane. Sparkling shards flew outward, showering onto the sloping porch roof.

Nancy stuck her head out the window and greedily gulped air into her lungs. It was warm and tangy, but at least it didn't have ether in it!

After wrapping her hand in the velvet curtain, she knocked the remaining splinters of glass out of the window frame. Then she crossed the room and stood over Chris Trout, who still hadn't budged. This part was going to be really hard.

"Okay, Mr. Trout, are you ready?" she asked him. He didn't answer.

"Shall I take that as a yes?" Nancy giggled, suddenly light-headed. "Well, ready or not, here I come—and here you go."

She stooped, grabbed Trout's limp arms, and hauled him up to a sitting position. His head lolled to one side. "Boy, you're a heavy sleeper," she chided him.

Twisting around so that her back was to him, she draped his arms over her shoulders and clasped her hands around his wrists. Then, slowly and laboriously, she began dragging him toward the open window. It was incredibly hard. Trout's muscular frame was heavier than it looked, and Nancy was already quite weak.

Suddenly she felt resistance. Looking down, she saw that one of Trout's dragging feet had gotten stuck between two pieces of furniture. Not now, Drew. You don't have the time or strength!

Nancy had to put him down to free him. She had such difficulty lifting him again that for a few dreadful moments she thought she might not be able to do it.

"Come on, Mr. Trout," she pleaded, gasping for breath. "Can't you help?" But he didn't stir.

Finally she got him onto her back again. Perspiring from the exertion, she lugged him the last few feet and draped his limp form over the windowsill. Then she reached for his feet and unceremoniously shoved him forward. He slid through the window and landed in a heap on the porch roof.

"Okay, me next," Nancy panted. She climbed through the window and out onto the roof. "Phase one complete," she murmured.

Next Nancy grabbed Trout by the feet and slid him down the gently sloping roof. It was easier than dragging him across the carpet, but Nancy was already thinking ahead to what had to come next. She wasn't certain she could handle it. Somehow she had to get him off the roof without breaking his neck—or her own—in the process.

Leaning over the edge of the roof, she peered down. Good. The drop didn't look to be more than eight or nine feet. Directly below her was the front lawn, and the grass looked soft and springy. That's the first thing that's gone right today, she thought with a wry smile.

She sat back and took a deep breath. Then she turned Trout over so that he was lying on his stomach with his feet pointing toward the edge of the roof.

Inch by inch she lowered him over the edge of the roof. At last, when his legs and lower torso were dangling, Nancy could no longer hold him. She let go, and he slid the rest of the way off the roof, landing in the grass with a thud.

Without pausing, Nancy sat on the edge of

the roof and then pushed off with her hands. She dropped heavily to the ground beside Trout.

Her muscles were aching, but she couldn't rest yet. She knew they were still too close to the house. If the attic was to go up now, they could still be seriously injured. Gritting her teeth, Nancy grasped Trout's hands and began to drag him away from the house, toward the thicket of trees and bushes that surrounded it.

They had crossed the driveway and were nearly at the trees when the explosion hit. A muffled thud came through the air from the attic. It sounded strangely soft, and at first Nancy didn't know what it was. Then the shock from the blast knocked her right off her feet, sending her sprawling in the grass. She threw her arms over her head to protect herself.

Peeking up, Nancy watched as the top of the Keatings' house erupted. It was as if the attic were a huge balloon that had been filled too full and had burst. Chunks of roof flew straight up into the air, and bits of wall blew out in every direction. Brick, mortar, and wood hailed down onto the lawn.

When the dust settled, Nancy saw that the entire upper half of the house was gone. Here and there orange flames shot up out of the ruins. She gulped. If we'd still been in there, she thought. If we hadn't gotten out . . .

Nancy started at the sound of a car door

slamming behind her. Had someone come to rescue them? Maybe Ned—

As she got to her feet and turned around, the welcoming words died on her lips.

Mr. Keating had come back! He stopped on the driveway, giving her a cold smile. "Miss Drew, isn't it?" When she nodded, he shook his head, and said, "It's a good thing I came back to check the damage. You keep popping up when I don't expect you," he said. "It was you on the bridge last night, wasn't it?"

Again Nancy nodded. She knew he planned to kill her. Her eyes darted around her, but she couldn't think of any way to escape. After what she'd been through, she knew she was far too weak to struggle against him.

Come on, Drew! her thoughts clamored. You just got yourself out of one of the worst messes you've ever been in. Surely you can come up with some way to outwit this goon. At least you can stall him until Trout comes around!

"Who'd have guessed, when you came to me for approval of that withdrawal the other day, that you'd be causing me so much trouble in such a short time?" Keating said, sighing.

Nancy raised her head and forced herself to smile. "I can be quite a troublemaker," she said, hoping she sounded more confident than she felt. "And I think you've already found out that I'm very hard to get rid of."

"Mmm, yes." Keating looked thoughtful. "I

don't know how you managed to get this far, but I do congratulate you. You're a resourceful girl."

Nancy didn't like his smug tone. He knew he had the upper hand, but she wasn't about to just buckle under. "Well, Mr. Keating," she said firmly, "it looks as if your plan has failed."

"Oh, I doubt that," Keating said coolly. He glanced up at the house. "No, I think the situation can still be repaired."

"How?" Nancy asked. She didn't really want to know, but she needed to keep distracting him.

"I saw enough in the war to know that the body of someone who's been in a fire is very difficult to identify. And there does seem to be a flame or two up there." Keating pointed up at the second story of the house. "I think I'll just put you back there and let nature take its course. It will be easy to claim your body as my wife's."

He turned toward her. Horrified, Nancy tried to back away, but the combination of fear and exhaustion had made her muscles utterly useless.

He was coming at her, and she couldn't move!

Chapter

Sixteen

Nancy stared helplessly as Mr. Keating began to cross the driveway toward her.

The sound of a car engine made her turn, and Nancy saw her blue Mustang roar up the drive, heading straight for Mr. Keating.

He leapt backward with a shout. "What the—?"

The Mustang's door flew open, and Mrs. Keating stepped out. Her gaze lit on Nancy, and Nancy thought she saw relief in the woman's eyes. Then Mrs. Keating turned to her husband and said in a shaking voice, "We can't do this, Bill."

"Listen to your wife, Mr. Keating," Nancy called to him. "She's trying to save you from a life behind bars."

Keating ignored her. "Maggie, what kind of

nonsense is this?" he demanded of his wife. "You know we can't stop now. We're in way too deep."

"No, Bill," Mrs. Keating pleaded. "You're wrong! If I let you kill these people, *then* it'll be too late. Cheating the insurance company was one thing, but I can't go along with murder!"

"You already have," Keating snapped. He gestured toward Nancy. "If this girl hadn't managed to get out before the house went up, you'd be an accessory after the fact right now. So don't get self-righteous with me."

Stepping around the car, he continued toward Nancy. She tensed, but she knew she couldn't hold him off for long—she was still too weak. "It's up to you, Mrs. Keating," she called. "You're the only one who can stop him from making the biggest mistake of his life."

"She won't stop me," Keating scoffed. "My wife is in this up to her neck."

Just then tires squealed on the Keatings' winding driveway, causing Mr. Keating to glance over his shoulder. A second later a green Chevy sedan came into sight. Ned!

As the car screeched to a halt, Nancy felt a rush of relief so intense that she thought her knees would buckle. As Ned leapt out of the car, Brenda's red sports car pulled up with Bess, George, Rick, and Brenda all crammed inside. All five of them raced over to Nancy.

"Am I glad to see you guys!" Nancy cried. But then, looking over Ned's shoulder, she saw the desperate look on Mr. Keating's face. In a flash he turned and started across the lawn at a run.

"Don't let him get away!" she cried, pointing.

Ned and Rick caught up to him in a flash and wrestled him to the ground. Keating's face twisted with fury. "You punks!" he growled, still struggling. Then Ned stunned him with a well-placed blow to the jaw.

As Keating went limp, Ned rubbed his fist and looked satisfied. "That was for last night," he said. Leaving Rick to handle his uncle, Ned rose to his feet and rushed back to Nancy, putting his arms around her. "Are you okay?" he asked tenderly.

Nancy hugged him as hard as she could. "How in the world did you know I'd be here?" she asked.

"I called your house, and Hannah told me you'd gone tearing out ten minutes earlier shouting something about stopping a murder," Ned told her. "Well, I know my Nancy," he went on, grinning affectionately. "I figured you had either gone here or to Brenda's. I called Brenda, and you weren't there, so that left here. So I told Brenda to call Bess and George for backup, and then I drove over. I want you to know I broke the speed limit all the way."

"I'm glad you did," Nancy said, giggling. She felt giddy now that she was out of danger, but she knew it wasn't over quite yet. Turning to Bess and George, she said, "Guys, there's some rope in the trunk of my car. Maybe we should tie Mr. Keating up, just in case he wakes up and wants to go somewhere."

"Okay, boss." George made a salute and headed for Nancy's Mustang. "I'll run to a neighbor's and call the fire department, too."

"Nan, you're kind of pale," Bess said anxiously. "Are you really all right?"

With a grateful smile Nancy assured her, "Now that you guys are here, I am." She looked over at Mrs. Keating, who was standing by herself next to Nancy's car.

"Mrs. Keating, I guess I owe you some thanks, too," Nancy said, going over to her. "If you hadn't had second thoughts, I probably wouldn't be standing here right now."

"Aunt Maggie!" Rick exclaimed, rushing to his aunt's side. "Hey, are you okay? He didn't hurt you, did he?"

Mrs. Keating glanced from her nephew to Nancy with a pale, blank expression. She looked as if she'd been carved from a block of ice.

"Aunt Maggie?" Rick repeated when she didn't answer. "Hey, what's the matter?"

Nancy cleared her throat. Suddenly she felt sad—sad for Rick, who was about to learn the awful truth about his favorite aunt, and even a little sad for Mrs. Keating herself.

"Rick," Nancy said softly. "I think your aunt has something to tell you."

"What do you mean?" Rick looked puzzled.

Instead of answering, Nancy looked expectantly at Mrs. Keating.

"All right!" Mrs. Keating burst out suddenly. "I'll tell him." She turned to Rick, her eyes filling with tears. "Your uncle wasn't trying to kill me, Rick," she explained in a shaky voice. "The whole thing was a scam, from beginning to end. Bill and I planned to fake my death in an accident, so that we could collect the insurance money and start fresh somewhere else."

A shocked silence fell over the group. Rick's jaw dropped, and he stared at his aunt.

Poor guy, Nancy thought with a pang. She was pleased when Brenda moved forward and took his hand without a word. Rick hardly seemed to notice. He just continued gazing at his aunt, a look of horror on his face.

"Don't stare at me like that," Mrs. Keating cried. She turned her back, and Nancy saw her shoulders heave with her sobbing.

After a moment she went on. "It was Bill's idea, but I didn't have to be talked into it," she said. "We both like spending money so much, there just never seemed to be enough of it—"

"Enough for what?" Rick asked in a low, bitter voice. "Uncle Bill has a good job! Why don't you just admit you were greedy?"

Mrs. Keating sighed. "All right, it's true. We *were* greedy. But we also had some problems. Bill had been trying to pad out his salary with some risky gambles on the stock market. A couple of those went sour, and we lost a lot. So he took a—a loan from his bank."

A loan? Nancy remembered how upset Keating had gotten when his secretary told him the bank's auditors were coming. "Mrs. Keating, do you mean your husband embezzled money from the bank?"

"Maggie, don't tell them anything!" came Mr. Keating's furious voice.

Turning, Nancy saw that he had come to, and was struggling against the ropes that bound his wrists and ankles. Ignoring him, Nancy repeated her question to Mrs. Keating.

The older woman glanced hesitantly at her husband. "Well, I—oh, what's the use! Yes, that's what I mean. He embezzled."

"I see," Nancy said with a nod. "Go on."

"At first we were going to stage a phony car accident. We were going to drive my car over the cliff and into the river. Then I'd disappear, and Bill would convince the authorities that I'd been in the car when it went over." Mrs. Keating shrugged. "The current was strong there. No one would question the fact that there was no body in the car."

"Ugh," Bess said softly. "That's creepy!"

Mrs. Keating looked at Brenda. "The day that I ran into you in the mall parking lot, I was trying to establish that my car had bad brakes," she explained. "I never thought you'd make such a fuss and draw so much attention to me, and I certainly never dreamed you'd put me in your column the next day."

"I'm a journalist," Brenda boasted. "It's my job to make things public."

"But Brenda made up that letter," Rick said to his aunt. "She didn't know anything."

Mrs. Keating nodded. "I know that now, but at the time all we could think of was that somehow she'd found out about our plan. Bill was furious. I was just scared—I wanted to call the whole thing off then and there, but he refused. He told me not to worry about it, that he'd make sure Brenda didn't talk." Her brown eyes were filled with shame as she added, "When Rick told me about Brenda's nearly being hit by the beam at the mall, I wondered if Bill had had anything to do with it, but I was afraid to ask."

"Did you, Mr. Keating?" Nancy called to him.

"What do you think?" Keating suddenly flared. "Of course! It was a piece of cake. My bank was one of the principal backers of the mall when it was built. I have the blueprints in my office—I know every inch of that place. I followed the girl there, and then I sneaked up to the roof by way of one of the catwalks and waited for her to walk under the broken skylight." His chest swelled with pride. "It was a calculated risk—but I've never been afraid of risks. I'm a winner."

"Most gamblers say the same thing," Nancy pointed out. "But they all lose sooner or later."

Keating just glared at her. After a moment Nancy turned back to Mrs. Keating. "Please go on with your story."

Mrs. Keating brushed back her ash blond hair and swallowed hard. "Well, after Brenda's column came out, things started happening fast," she said. "Bill told me that the bank auditors were coming in to do an investigation. We thought they might discover the missing money, and we couldn't let that happen. So we had to speed up our timetable. If I 'died' over the weekend, then Bill would have a plausible reason to be out of work next week. Without him the audit couldn't be held, and the auditors would have to reschedule, probably to sometime in the fall—that's the way these people work. And by that time we'd be long gone with the insurance money."

"Devious," Ned said, shaking his head.

"Yes, but the problem was that on Friday afternoon the mechanic from the garage where we'd had the car towed called to say that they'd discovered one of the brake shoes was missing."

"Ah!" Nancy said softly. "Enter Chris Trout." She was pretty sure she knew what was coming next.

Mrs. Keating nodded. "Right. Shortly after that, my brother-in-law showed up at our door," she said. "He had the missing brake shoe, and he knew it had been filed down. He'd pretty much figured out what we were trying to do. He said he wouldn't tell anyone about it—as long as we gave him half the insurance money, once we got it.

"Our plans were falling apart," Mrs. Keating went on. Nancy had the impression that it was actually a relief to her to confess everything. "It was too risky to try the phony car accident—the mechanic knew my car had been tampered with. But we had to try something. Chris was pressuring us for money. We didn't know what to do—until this morning, when we heard there was a tornado watch."

"I heard that report, too," Nancy told her.

"Bill had been keeping a file of clippings on microbursts—he's very interested in natural phenomena," Mrs. Keating said. "I think he'd been turning over the possibility of staging a phony microburst for some time. At any rate, he knew how to do it. It seemed our problems were solved."

"Until I turned up," Nancy guessed.

"Not exactly. Chris came about ten minutes before you, to push us about the money," Mrs. Keating corrected Nancy, nodding toward Trout's still-unconscious form. "Bill knocked him out and took him up to the study. *Then* you came along."

"And you knocked me out, too, figuring that

when the blast was over, the authorities would find our remains, and everyone would think that I was you," Nancy concluded.

Mrs. Keating nodded. "But I couldn't go along with that," she whispered. "I couldn't."

"Maybe that will help you in court, Aunt Maggie," Rick said.

There was an uneasy silence. Finally, after a long moment, Nancy spoke up. "Well, I suppose one of us should go call the police. With Mrs. Keating's confession, and all these witnesses, I don't think we'll have much trouble proving this case."

"Just think," Brenda gloated. "If it hadn't been for me, we never would have stumbled on this case in the first place!"

Nancy rolled her eyes. Rick's whole family was falling apart, and Brenda could think only about herself!

But Brenda seemed to have realized her own mistake. She was actually looking remorseful. "I'm sorry," she said softly to Rick. "I didn't mean it to sound that way. I wasn't thinking."

Rick's face softened, and he smiled down at her. "I know you didn't mean it," he said. With a deep sigh he added, "I'm just glad to finally know the truth. And at least Aunt Maggie's still alive."

"I guess that's what really counts," Brenda told him, giving Rick a sympathetic smile.

Nancy grinned. Maybe Brenda *would* learn!

* * *

"Well, Brenda," Nancy said after the police had taken all their statements and carted the Keatings and Chris Trout away, "I think we can drop the contest about whose summer is more exciting. We're even now, at two attacks apiece—and I, for one, would rather not compete anymore!"

"Hear, hear!" George cried.

"Yeah, I hate competition," Bess put in.

Ned laughed. "I have an idea. I say we all just concentrate on having as much fun as possible this summer."

"That's the best idea you've had in a long time," Nancy declared. Then she kissed him.

Nancy's next case:

Nancy and her pals have come to rustic Oakwood Inn to indulge in a chocolate-festival fantasy. Add a dash of Brock Sawyer—celebrity taster and one of TV's hottest stars—and you have the makings of a perfect weekend. But the sweet dream turns sour when Brock is rushed to the hospital—poisoned!

Brock's ex-girlfriend, Samantha Patton, is running the show, and Nancy discovers that there's venom aplenty behind the scenes. Greed, ambition, and jealousy are the sinister ingredients in a bitter new recipe for revenge. Nancy must catch the crooked cook before murder brings the pot to a boil . . . in *SWEET REVENGE*, Case #61 in The Nancy Drew Files™.

The Linda Stories

*Read all about the boys
in Linda's life...
from her first crush to
the ups and downs of
a powerful true love.*

☐ *We Hate Everything But Boys*   72225/$2.95
When Linda and her friends start the We Hate Everything But Boys club, watch out! They'll do *anything* to
find out if the boys they like really like them, too.
Have four boy-crazy girls ever caused so much trouble?

☐ *Is There Life After Boys*   69559/$2.95
It's a new year and Linda's at a new school...full of
girls! In the meantime, back at P.S. 515, Sue-Ann is
putting the moves on Linda's boyfriend! The situation
seems hopeless until Linda meets Mark and discovers
something wonderful...there's nothing like an older
boy to mend a broken heart!

☐ *We Love Only Older Boys*   69558/$2.95
Linda loves Louie...that's what's tattooed all over
Linda's heart. If only Louie would decide *he* loves
her! Linda's best friends already have older boy-
friends, but all *she's* got is boy trouble. Then Linda
discovers the perfect solution to her problems—right
under her nose!

continued

☐ *My Heart Belongs To That Boy*   70353/$2.95
When Linda and Lenny first get together, it's *wonderful*.
This is real love, at last! But then Lenny starts cutting
school and flirting with other girls, and the fireworks
start! Linda still loves him, but she can't help but
wonder...how will they ever get it right?

☐ *All For The Love Of That Boy*   68243/$2.95
After a summer apart, Linda is sure she and Lenny will
never break up again. It's great to be back with her old
crowd, and back in Lenny's arms again...until her
friends start drifting apart, and Lenny pulls his craziest
stunt ever. With everything changing so fast, will their
love change, too?

☐ *Dedicated To That Boy I Love*   68244/$2.75
By senior year Linda knows it's true—Lenny is the love
of her life. Even if he *does* still get into trouble
sometimes, Linda is determined to stand by him. But
then when Lenny finally finds a way to get his act
together for good, Linda's world is turned completely
upside down!

☐ *Loving Two Is Hard To Do*   70587/$2.95
Linda doesn't set out to have a summer romance...it
just happens. Dave is handsome and smart, and he
never gets into trouble like Lenny. Soon Linda is back
in the city, though, and so is Lenny. She can't have
them both...but how can she ever choose
between them?